"The desert group has changed its position in the night and is moving toward the city. Around the park, the military police have been posted, prepared to control the traffic. This is it, the day of destiny, the day of triumph.

"It is there in the desert that the operation's heart is beating, while I, looking across the city here, am just the brain. I remember the walls of that space school building and the skeleton of the rocket gantry that was rising at the time in the desert valley. Men moving on those barren hills, not knowing what they did or why, except that they had my orders.

"These people, waking and rising in the city, do not know what day this is.

"The rocket should be turning over in the sky now. I visualize it, checking its momentum and preparing to swoop down on Arcon, much quicker to fall than it was to go up and leave us. And the city waits, unknowing."

REX GORDON

has also written:

FIRST ON MARS

FIRST TO THE STARS

FIRST THROUGH TIME

UTOPIA MINUS X

the Yellow Fraction

REX GORDON

AN ACE BOOK

Ace Publishing Corporation
1120 Avenue of the Americas
New York, N.Y. 10036

THE YELLOW FRACTION

Cover art by Kelly Freas

I

SOMETHING HAD TO HAPPEN, Len Thomas thought. Things were getting so tight that something had to happen soon.

Len Thomas walked across the blue-tinged grass. There were two suns in the Arcon sky, but Len did not worry about that. It was more a feeling, a feeling that had been with him before this started. Yet the feeling was largely incoherent.

Like falling over his own feet, for example.

He looked as homely and ordinary as his name suggested, and he went into the glass-bubble part of the building, the top part of which looked like an inverted pyramid on a silver stalk, and he pushed his name-card recognition tag into the slot in the computer-director just inside the door.

Arcon life. Arcon student life. How was it possible to see a brain that had grown up on Arcon? Worse than that, how was it possible for such a brain to see itself? Len didn't. It was only sometimes that he even tried.

He did what he had to do. Two loudspeakers on top of the building, speakers that had been whispering "Leonard Thomas report to Administration," became silent when he put his nametag into the computer-director and it digested it. Outside through the glass, the blue-tinged grass, which must have been green once, but which was now definitely blue, lay dry and arid in the bright, double-spectrum light of the two suns.

A crowd of other students was always leaving or entering the glass foyer. A screen on the computer-director came alight. THOMAS REPORT TO INFORMATION, it said. Two girl students, passing along the line of office computers, said "Hello, Len," as they went by.

Our way is right, and all others wrong.

How could any young man know anything but the planet, the civilization, that had given him birth? Who was going to start to question what everyone-who-ought-to-know-said? If other people in other places or at other times lived in different ways, then they were wrong, and that applied regardless of what their society was: sophisticated, civilized, or headhunting.

A young male student took a little longer to pass. He

looked at the computer-director screen. He glanced at Len, and then at the message that was still glowing as Len acknowledged it on the keyboard. He laughed in a voice that gave Len a considerable lack of pleasure. "What have you been doing?" he said. Len did not answer him.

Len feared he knew what he had been doing but, in that case, so did the other student.

Arcon was a pot about to boil. Len did not know why he felt that. Maybe it was him. Maybe it was what all young men felt, always. Or could it be what was felt by a foolish young man in trouble?

He went down the ranks of office computers until he reached the one marked INFORMATION OFFICE. He behaved differently there. It was not a popular computer. While most of the others had a student or two banging away at their keyboards, making dates with tutors, or filing their exercises, or explaining why they had not done their mathematics, the one with the INFORMATION OFFICE sign was shunned as though it had a smell around it. Len treated it that way too.

He typed his name on the keyboard and pushed his nametag into the slot to confirm it, and then stood back.

It was possible that some nice kindly message might someday emerge from an Information Office computer, but if so that was something that had not happened to Len yet.

What the I. O. computer usually said was something like "Male students should be out of girls' rooms by 8 P.M." or "Orphans are expected to make special efforts for longer living," or something equally natural, which required an answer that would be found in the computer's memory-banks.

Len knew, and feared, that the computer could also exact penalties. He waited to see what would happen to him. The computer screen lit up. THOMAS LEONARD, ATTEND ROOM 202B, IMMEDIATE, it said. Len stared. He stood looking at the screen like someone already on a diet, looking at the pointer of a weighing machine that had just gone off the scale.

The male student had wandered around the glass foyer of the Administration building. Apparently by accident, he was not far behind Len when the words appeared on the screen. He too looked at them with interest. "You seem to have had it, chum," he said to Len. Then he walked off to where the other students were, to tell other people.

They all looked at Len, too.

It was not a bad analogy, a weighing-machine pointer

going off the scale, when the Information Office computer referred its correspondent to Floor Twenty, as it was in the college's case, for human intervention. Len suddenly saw the message change from blue to red, and he typed his confirmation hurriedly.

He looked in the direction of the other students, then pointedly looked away again. He did not like the way they were watching him as he walked across the foyer to the central silver stalk that held up the building. The silver stalk was also the elevator shaft. In front of its smooth door, he pushed the button for an elevator to Floor Twenty. The door opened almost immediately, and closed behind him as he stepped into the small, airless elevator compartment.

"The bastard," Len said to himself as he rode up in the elevator. "The wealthy blue-nosed bastard." He was reflecting on the student who was no doubt talking and laughing with the others he had gone to, who belonged to the Blue and Green fraternities. Len had not long to reflect on anything. The elevator door opened and he was contemplating a silent corridor with smooth doors and a deep well-fitted carpet.

There was an absence of people in the corridor, and the overhead lighting was soft and calm. When Len walked soundlessly on the carpet and knocked on the door marked 202B, he noticed that it, like the other doors, had no handle. Involuntarily, he took a breath while he waited.

If anyone said "Come in" behind the door, he did not hear them, but the door opened of its own accord, and he faced a pleasant, calm room with a youngish man in a pale gray suit sitting at a large desk in front of a considerable downward-facing window which gave a view of the college. In front of the desk was an empty chair, and in answer to a gesture from the pale-faced, slightly overweight young man Len went to sit in it.

The door closed behind him. Len did not see the man behind the desk press a button to close it, but perhaps he did, or maybe there was some other way of doing it.

"Leonard Thomas?" the young man said. He had very clean white hands, and one of them rested on a file marked *L. Thomas*, which lay on the desk in front of him.

"Yes, sir," Len said, not knowing what to expect next.

"It was you who organized that petition that has been circulating?" the man said with an appearance of frankness. "The one asking that the recent history lecturer, Gordon Berkeley, should be reinstated?" He used a cool tone.

Len hesitated a fraction of a second. He thought of the student below, who had probably told how he had been approached to sign a petition, and by whom. "Yes, sir," he said. He knew that that was it, then.

The man on the other side of the desk continued to smile in an apparently friendly way. Len was not deceived by the friendliness. The man said, "My name is Gorlston."

"Yes, Mr. Gorlston," Len said.

"The lecturer Berkeley was dismissed by us," the man called Gorlston remarked, as though it were an interesting fact that Len should know. "His lectures were politically unreliable. They had a Yellow taint."

By "us," Mr. Gorlston evidently meant the Information Office. The remark about the Yellow taint of the lectures was enough to make that clear.

Len was caught. He had been organizing a petition for Berkeley's reinstatement. "They seemed perfectly good lectures to me, sir," he said.

Gorlston stopped smiling. He looked at Len as though Len had suddenly taken things onto a new level of seriousness. "Then maybe you are a Yellow too," he said.

Len's eyes opened wider. "Oh no, sir. I'm not."

The conversation was beginning to progress the way such conversations had to progress on Arcon, paranoiacally.

Gorlston looked at Len thoughtfully. He made a remark as though it were something a little delicate: "You are if I say so," he said.

Len looked down at the desk, thinking how true that was. He himself had never knowingly met a Yellow in his life. But then you could not expect a Yellow to say he was a Yellow. The Information Office would have removed him if he had done that. So only the Information Office knew who the Yellows were. It came around in a circle to the fact that if an Information Officer said Len was a Yellow, then Len was a Yellow.

It was hard to think of anyone being a Yellow voluntarily.

"If you are not a Yellow, how would you describe yourself?"

"Loyal Arcon."

Did he think that was going to do any good?

"Which party?"

Len remembered Berkeley saying that you did not have to belong to the official parties to be a loyal citizen, but that was Berkeley, and look where it had got him.

Gorlston was waiting.

8

"I haven't quite made up my mind between the Greens and Blues."

He might as well give up now.

Gorlston looked his opinion of a final year student who could not make up his mind between the Greens, who said that Arcon would be transformed into a green and pleasant land, and the Blues, who said that Arcon was a blue planet and man would have to adapt to it. Swamp-diggers made that choice, and little children waving flags as they followed the bands at the National Party conventions.

Women, and girls who had just got the vote, and the mentally deficient who could only write a cross.

"So," said Gorlston.

How could you be a loyal Arcon if you were not prepared to do something by voting along one of the regular channels? What did you think you were going to do, figure something out for yourself that was better than the national leaders could?

"Mr. Gorlston," said Len.

He had better say something. He had left it a little late as it was. How to do it without pleading and crawling was another matter. Maybe that was not possible.

"I know I am in trouble over that petition," he said simply. "How do I get out of it?"

Gorlston stared at Len as though he thought he was kidding him. Maybe no one on Arcon had tried to be as simple as that with an Information Officer before.

Then Gorlston's eyes narrowed. Len had asked a question, and if Len wanted it like that, he could have it.

"You can go back to the students you approached about the petition. You can tell them, for example, that you and Berkeley had a homosexual relationship." Gorlston's eyes went down to Len's file on his desk. It was probably a complete file, which would tell him that since Len's parents' death he was completely dependent on the authorities for financial backing.

"That's why you wanted him reinstated," Gorlston said.

Len thought about it.

Homosexuality was not popular on Arcon. After five hundred years of planetary history there were still traces of that pioneering morality that looked with horror on any kind of sexual deviation that did not result in children, but it was not exactly that.

Maybe it was just staying something about Berkeley that was untrue.

"I think you're wrong, Mr. Gorlston," Len said carefully.

9

"I mean I think you're wrong now because you were right earlier. It could be that I am a Yellow."

It was unpleasant to be a Yellow on Arcon. Len did not know just how unpleasant. He had not liked to imagine it.

But it was not that; it was the stigma. It was being what being a Yellow meant, on Arcon. How could a man brought up on Arcon ever tell himself he was a Yellow?

II

ARCON WAS the thirty-seventh and only habitable planet of a binary star, and it pursued a long and irregular orbit around its solar system. It was this which had caused the men who had colonized it, five hundred years before, to retain the Earth-style calendar. A three-lifetime year was too long.

It was interesting to know that this was one of the few things which could not be blamed on the Yellows.

What Arcon was could be laid at the door of the founding fathers, who, out of the whole of space, had chosen it to live on. It was possible that they could be criticized, but like most men they could have made excuses.

The truth was that the crew of the starship from Earth had been space-weary when they came to Arcon. It was no joke, after setting out to find a better world, to discover that most worlds, as average planets of average stars, were red-hot rocks, or balls of frozen gas. *Another world*, a diary said. *We are beginning to get used to it now, this process of blasting down, then blasting up to speed again. Methane and ammonia, and the last cool-enough world was chlorine. . . .*

They should have known what to expect. They did.

While stars could be seen ahead for immense distances in space, at that time the planets could only be examined on arrival, when passing slowly through a solar system. In those days it was necessary to go from star to star, wondering increasingly if habitable worlds were less frequent than had been supposed.

Star voyages were never simple things for the early pioneers. They set out from Earth and accelerated upward, toward the speed of light. That was straightforward enough. The stars ahead glowed bright blue, those astern became a dull red, and the universe shrank around them. There was nothing odd about these phenomena, which were the natural consequences of the Doppler effect and the mass-accretion of bodies traveling at near speed-of-light speeds, but those who were not good at mathematics, and who were not really at home with relativity, distrusted them on the grounds that they could not wholly understand them.

It was the knowledge that after the first of those shifts, and just an ordinary few weeks' passage through the diminished universe, that time passed at a different rate at home, and that everyone they knew was now dead, which somehow produced effects that were psychological. No one could say that star-travelers were actually guilty, or that they had exceeded their normal life-span in some cheating way, but, after a few such passages from star to star, during which time centuries were known to have rolled away at home, the psychological sensation was one of doom. It was not a reasoned thing. The fact remained that the next star would probably produce a habitable world, or perhaps the next. There were no grounds for thinking that they would wander forever, finding nowhere to land until they died of old age. But that was the way they felt about it.

So when they did come out of the continuum, and arrived in the near vicinity of a star, to see a world like Arcon, with a blue-iridescent and slightly dazzling quality in its atmosphere, turning away below them, there was a kind of anguished impulse to land on it, to make the best of what they had got, to have done with the dread of space, and end the journey.

It was not that the ancestors of Len and his people, who had populated and built a quite considerable civilization on Arcon in five hundred years, had been wholly reckless or unscientific. They would not have survived at all if they had been. It was just that, arriving at Arcon's suns, and seeing Arcon below them, and when the first gross measurements proved favorable—gravity point nine of Earth, oxygen in the atmosphere, radiation at the surface at least such that they would not get cancer within hours of landing—a conviction and certainty grew in them that this was the place, which was not easily upset by the later final details of spectroscopy.

What actually happened among the crew and colonists, while their ship hung above the beautiful world below them, was, like so many things, a matter of unchangeable history by Len's time.

After all, the colonists and crew, dividing into factions as the rumors reached them inside the metal walls and down the passageways of the town-sized starship, only

11

thought they were arguing the immediate practical matter of whether to land or not. Since social psychology was still in its primitive state, they did not know they were laying down the foundations for political parties with their factions, or creating a human structure that would still run the world five hundred years later. They just evolved, quite naturally, three points of view.

"Look," one group said, arguing with the others in the corridors and public rooms while waiting for the final results from the scientists, "this is a well-equipped ship and colonial expedition. Be reasonable. In case of an emergency landing, we are equipped to deal with almost everything, provided the gravity and air is such that we can walk about and breathe. We must have confidence in ourselves. What we have to do is go down there, and show what we can do. We aren't so superstitious as to expect ghouls in the night or bug-eyed monsters, and what we have to do, regardless of the final details, is to turn this world into a green and pleasant land for man to live on."

They were naturally known as the Green faction, when the question of landing was put to the final and infallible democratic procedure of the vote.

The Blues said, "On the whole we agree with the Greens. That is, if we go on searching through space for perfection forever, we'll never find it. But some of the scientists' findings are pretty poor. They relate to the biochemical factors, and biochemistry is a very complicated science. So while we agree we should land on Arcon, we are a bit more cautious about it. The way we see it is that Arcon is a blue planet, and it will stay that way. But this we do say, that mankind will adapt to it."

The Blues and the Greens were therefore agreed on landing, and between them they were the great majority.

But because it had worked out that way, and the faction that talked of turning Arcon into a green and pleasant land were called the Greens, and the faction that talked of mankind's adapting to a blue planet were called the Blues, then the minority, who were against the landing, had to be given a name that damned them.

They were called the Yellows.

III

LIFE WAS different on Arcon after five hundred years. There was a people for one thing, instead of a community, and manufacturing industries and commerce had grown up in the great cities by the shallow seas.

There was a political structure, and a government, and national and local institutions, a senate, and organizations that came down from the national to the local level, and produced their results in homes and shops and offices, amid the results of what had become known as the Arcon style of architecture.

For example, there was the downward-facing window behind Gorlston's head.

Gorlston looked at Len thoughtfully across the desk with the view and the light behind him. "I don't think you quite realize what you're saying, Thomas, when you say you may be a Yellow."

Did Len? He did not know. He had been born on Arcon, in its five-hundred-year civilization, and he could not escape its standards.

"I think I know what the Yellows are, Mr. Gorlston. And, believe me, I don't want to be named a Yellow."

On Arcon, a Yellow could not be employed, nor could he get public relief.

"Tell me," Gorlston said.

Len hated to do it for some reason. It seemed to him too easy, when everyone knew the case against them, to condemn the Yellows.

"The Yellows are the anti-Arcon party. They've been against our Arcon government and Arcon civilization since the early days. All the great troubles we have had on Arcon are said to be due to the Yellows, who caused them by their sabotage. It was first said they were causing trouble when the First Agricultural Program went to pieces after forty years."

Len realized his mistake after he had said it. It was just exactly what someone who had attended Berkeley's lectures would do. Instead of saying the troubles were due to the Yellows, he had said they were *said* to be due to the Yellows.

It sounded like a small thing, that conditional view of truth, but Len knew that by his job Gorlston would see it as a mistake, and that instead of recovering himself and improving his position with Gorlston, Len was losing points.

Outside the window, and in the area all around them that Len could see, the college was going on with its normal life. But Len felt cut off from it while talking to Gorlston. Why did he have something of the feeling of a small boy again, talking to a heavy-handed teacher, in the junior grade?

Maybe he was playing for bigger stakes than small boys usually played for.

"Go on," Gorlston said.

"You want me to go on talking about the Yellows?"

"Yes."

If you want to know, I've had some sympathy for the Yellows, just because everyone is down on them, and as far as I'm concerned they have been invisible. Len didn't say it.

How did they feel, with everyone's hand against them?

"The airlines had crashes." Better not say what he thought. "That must have been later. The government had to take over transport and communications. That was how we got the army. In case the settlements revolted. Then it was because of the disaster period, when we became an industrial society, that the Information Office had to be set up, to seek out the Yellows."

Gorlston had a clean, well-fed face, and a white collar. "I've heard third-grade students give me a better history of the Yellows than you are giving me," he said to Len.

Len was not surprised.

"Maybe that's true." He wished he could remember not to be tart. "Third-grade students would have it by heart, since it would be in their examination that year."

Golrston looked speculative.

Gorlston looked like an angler who had gone fishing. He had to set bait to catch a fish like Len.

"While you have forgotten your history?"

Len sat where he was and tried not to wriggle on the hook.

"Not since Mr. Berkeley, sir."

Gorlston opened Len's file and turned the pages, pointing. "You are a final-year science and technology student. Mathematics and electronics. So why did you go back to history?"

Len blushed.

"Science students don't like history, do they?" Gorlston said calmly. "Dead stuff, past events, boring speeches. Isn't that the view you people take of it?"

"It was a girl, sir," Len said. "A girl called June. There was this new history lecturer. You remember, sir? It was pushed." Len's eyes opened wider. "Everyone should go to them. June said she was going, and would I go with her."

"This girl, June," Gorlston said. "She kept up with the course? She attended all the lectures and signed your petition at the end?"

14

Len looked away at the corner of the room. "No, sir. Not many students stayed to the end. June found Mr. Berkeley a little coarse."

"Coarse?"

Len struggled with what he tried to remember of the incident.

"I think it was when Mr. Berkeley talked about the so-called Perfect World, sir. That is, the civilization that existed on Earth before our people left it. Mr. Berkeley said that affairs on Earth were supposed to be so well arranged that people had nothing to do but make conversation and play games and make love all day. That's why additives had to be added to the water supply so they didn't have children except when the additives were stopped, which was always at three P.M. on Tuesdays.

"And?"

"I laughed, sir. June didn't."

In fact, June had been furious.

"So you think it is funny, when a man who is supposed to be a responsible lecturer jokes about the Progenitive Right of Man, which is one of the reasons our ancestors left Earth for Arcon?"

Was it? Reading through the lines of Berkeley's lectures, you came to doubt it.

"I think it was Mr. Berkeley's personality, sir."

"That excused him?"

"He was bright, sir. Bright and witty. Sometimes bitter. Sometimes his lectures seemed superficial, sir, but at the same time shrewd, a good man."

Gorlston looked hard at Len. "Maybe I was right," he said. "Maybe there was something in this suggestion of a homosexual relationship between yourself and Berkeley."

Len felt sick.

"You had talks with him, didn't you? He lent you books?"

It would not have been much advantage to Len to attend the lectures if he had not got as far as that with his tutor.

"It's a lie, sir."

"Do you know your June told me that when she told you to choose between her and Berkeley, you chose Berkeley?"

June? Where did June come into this?

"Your June is in very good standing with the Information Office," Gorlston said. "You should be the same."

Len had known that some students made a point of working with the Information Office. But June? June was the one who had taken him to Berkeley's lectures, then stayed away. . . .

"It helps," Gorlston said. "For example, when you leave the college. You know you will be leaving the college shortly, don't you? Employers don't like people with a low Information Office rating. They don't employ them, for patriotic reasons."

Such as that if an employer did employ someone with a low I.O. rating, he would soon get a low I.O. rating himself, and get no government contracts.

Not merely would he get no government contracts himself, but a bigger firm that employed him as a sub-contractor would get no government contracts either.

"I'm leaving the college shortly, sir?"

Not before the final examinations, surely.

"We can't have homosexuals in the college," Gorlston said. "Neither among the staff nor with the students."

It began to look as though it did not matter if Len told that story or someone else did.

June, perhaps?

"If I don't pass the exam, sir . . . !"

"There are more important things in life than examination results," Gorlston said. "Such as your Information Office rating."

How true that was.

"But, sir—"

"But when we quietly got rid of Berkeley, you had to start to make a fuss and raise a hornet's nest about him. You've got to put that right."

Len wondered wildly if he could say he had caught Berkeley stealing the silver teaspoons, or something comparatively innocuous. But for what? To save himself? The last person anyone seemed to be considering in this was Berkeley.

"I won't do it, sir."

"You'd prefer to be dismissed as a homosexual *and* be given a Yellow rating?"

Len gulped.

He tried to foresee a future for himself, in a competitive society, with a double burden. How he would eat, for example? How did Yellows eat? Anyone giving them a handout would be automatically classed a Yellow.

"Sir—"

"You're a fool. Do you know that?"

Don't tell me. I've been suspecting it for a long time.

A Yellow fool. Len looked out of the window. Did all

16

the people in the college out there know they were standing on their heads? Or was that just the effect of looking
at the world upward, from the underside?

"If that's all you can say for yourself, you can go," said
Gorlston.

Len stood up. He was surprised to be told he could go.
If he was a Yellow, weren't they going to arrest him then
and there?

"And pack," said Gorlston. "Just go to your room and
wait there." He moved his hand very slightly on his desk,
and on Len's left the door swung open. Len went for it.
These electronic desks were wonderful.

"Don't leave the college," Gorlston said.

Len was outside in the corridor, looking at the elevator,
which was waiting for him. Was he not under guard? Was
no one going to accompany him to his room, and see he
did not leave the college?

It did cross his mind that Gorlston might just possibly
be giving him a chance to do something desperate. But
what? Suicide?

Len headed for the elevator with some determination.
Who did the Information Office and the Blues and Greens
think they were, anyway? Len headed for the outer world,
for life, such as it was, on the planet Arcon.

IV

LIFE ON ARCON was human, and as such it contained many
echoes. The distances were enormous, and the planets were
different, but wherever Man went in the cosmos there would
be variety, and numbers of complications, and the con-
flict of different people. No history could be seen exclusively in Yellow, or for that matter in Green or Blue terms.

No history was ever balanced. No historian was ever what
he hoped to be, objective. As well might an historian,
way back on Earth, be asked to write a history of the
Buddha, when he was a follower of the Prophet. No atheist
could tell the story of the early Christian churches, and
no follower of one church would not be disputed by all
the rest.

Documents were the raw material of history. Documents
were always the truth of history. Yet documents were only
the truth for the man who wrote them:

The Diary of J. Adolf Koln

The diary of J. Adolf Koln is especially interesting because the General was appointed commander of the Arcon First Army in the early sixth century After Landing. His command carried a seat on the General Staff and an office in the Hexagon in Davis City, and he was in a central position in world affairs at the time of the Rocket Project, which was Len Thomas' era.

June 3, 502 A.L.
I think I can say I am a patriot. Whether the word is applied to a country, a people or a planet, it means the same thing. In my mind it has a special meaning and a special feeling. For this reason I must try to be worthy of the magnitude of my new appointment.

June 9, 502 A.L.
I must define the reasons why I have begun to keep this journal. What do I see around me in my world of Arcon? I see the army, ordered, disciplined, and ever ready to do what it has to do. Beyond the army, I see civilians, neither ordered nor disciplined, all seeking their own advantage and pulling in all directions. It grieves me that there should be such a difference between the Service to which I have given my life and the civilian population, who are the ones we serve. On moving to the capital to take up my new appointment I will see commercial and political life at first hand. I will test my conclusion that this planet is corrupt. Ultimately, I may have to do something about this.

June 13, 502 A.L.
What should a general do, when he is bound by his oath of loyalty to a group of politicians whom he knows to be self-seeking and lacking both principles and honor? There must be an answer to this sense of frustration that is my feeling. I must think of it profoundly.

The diaries of J. Adolf Koln, with similar entries, are just one of the documents at which the would-be historian of Arcon should glance from time to time. They were not without their relevance, though overshadowed by the Information Office files, the archives of Arcon (which was a private collection), *The Jottings of G. Berkeley,* and sometimes, though with every caution, the standard histories of Arcon, which were best when dealing with generalities or ancient times, since they could only be written long afterward, when opinions at the time were always so misleading.

V

From *The Short History of Arcon:*

When the starship landed on Arcon, after the argument that had been settled by the legitimate democratic procedure of the vote, it became apparent at once that the Yellows had been wrong, and that either the Blues or Greens, or both, had been quite right. People did not merely walk out of the starship onto Arcon. They ran and jumped, and enjoyed themselves in their new surroundings, breathing healthy air.

It was natural that the most elaborate precautions were taken, and that all substances on Arcon were analyzed, before, for example, anyone was allowed to drink the water. Contrary to the Yellows' warnings, no poisonous substances were found, however. It was true that the chemistry of Arcon was different. There was an excess of iridium and tantalum, and a lack of iron. Many new compounds were in evidence, especially in the biochemical sphere, but the expedition, running up its dwellings, exploring a seashore, and laying out the ground plan of a town on a site found by a William Davis, proved exceptionally fortunate. The new compounds were present in almost everything, but they substituted well for Earth compounds, allowed crops to flourish when grown from Earth-type seed, and were stable, and, as far as could be seen for many years, non-toxic.

The experiment of allowing laboratory animals to live on the local produce first, before humans did, was quite successful. Inevitably they were small animals that lived short lives, but this allowed it to be demonstrated that they thrived and reproduced themselves.

Arcon therefore was a planet intended for human occupation. It lacked insects, and the laboratory insects died, but this was thought on the whole a good thing. The colonists had been more concerned that the laboratory insects should not escape and infest the planet, than that they should live long lives. The physical features of Arcon were found to be its deserts, which were wild and vast and dusty; the dust that was frequently in the higher atmosphere, explaining its iridescence; and also, fortunately, its shallow inland seas. A fairly rich indigenous flora and fauna were found in the primeval swamp-lands that surrounded the shallow seas, and the most dangerous life-form was found to be a swamp-frog, about nine inches long, which could spit a jet of poison that could penetrate the skin like a tiny dart. A disproportionate amount of energy and resources had to be expended in combating this insignificant swamp-frog.

The starship was kept up for a while, despite the calls for its machinery and constituent metals. It was not felt safe to dismantle it, at least until the first generation of children had been born, and proved to be normal, vigorous, and healthy. Scientific investigation of the environment was continued, and certain of the relatively new compounds common on Arcon were found to be a fairly effective insecticide.

The Blue faction remained cautious, pointing out that there had been long-term effects from certain insecticides that had been used on Earth, though agreeing that, whatever the differences in the environment were, men would ultimately adapt to them. The Green faction was joyful, insisting that everything was straightforward, and that already, with Earth grass growing, Arcon was on the way to becoming a green and pleasant land. A slight bluing of the edges of the grass was a minor effect, and of no consequence. The Yellows were not heard of at this time. If they thought anything, they kept it to themselves.

The starship was stripped down after twenty years on Arcon, when the first grandchild of an original settler was born, and proved to be whole and healthy. It was suggested that it would be good to keep the starship intact for sentimental reasons, but though the planet was not deficient in metals and the use of the new alloys would in time be successful, the expanding rural economy demanded iron in the early stages. Also the atomic generators of the starship were badly needed as a source of power. Altogether, a lot of people had been looking at the starship with acquisitive eyes for a long time, and when the order was given it was stripped and cannibalized very rapidly. A few Yellows objected then, but no one took any notice.

The first people, the original settlers on Arcon, lived a few years more, then died.

The second generation, then aged forty downward, said, "Fancy Mom and Pop dying at sixty. That's young. The star journey must have taken more out of them than we ever realized. Pity we didn't do more for them when they were alive."

But not all of the first settlers died at sixty, only those who had been younger than twenty when the starship

20

landed. Others, who had been older then, lived to greater ages, and for a while that obscured the pattern.

The next generation, the first to be born on Arcon, began to die off at forty. That was when autopsies began to be held, and concern expressed. A lot of concern. It was something to do with the accumulation of salts in the body over a long period. But this first generation was not very scientific. It had been more important to teach trades and skills like farming, and science could be kept and held safe in books. Besides, people at forty were pretty old anyway, by the ditch-digging and farming standards of young people who had a lot of children.

As for the grandchildren, and the third and fourth generations, they tended to feel that if people died at forty, then that was the way life was.

VI

Revolt.

Could a young man, knowing so little, revolt against what he did know? Len was surprised to find himself in the elevator, going down again to the foyer of the Administration building.

He had expected that Gorlston would either clear him, arrange a course of action for him, or arrest him then and there. Go to his college rooms, get his bags packed, and wait there, Gorlston had said. He might as well have told him to put his head in a guillotine and watch the knife descending.

Len thought it was a mistake on Gorlston's part to free him and send him to his rooms alone. He thought that Gorlston had thought he would be obedient.

He went down the the glass foyer and emerged among the office computers and the crowd of students. He was tempted to rebel there. He thought of yelling to the crowd of students: "You know the Information Office? How they pretend to be for rightness and justice, and for the good of Arcon? Well, it's a fraud."

Len had a little sense. He was learning more.

The male student who had watched Len go up in the elevator was waiting there on his return. His expression was interested and anticipatory, and he ran his tongue across his lips a little.

"How did you get on, and what did they say to you?"

"No comment," Len said, and walked straight toward the exit from the foyer.

21

The expression on the student's face had made it clear to Len that there was no future addressing a crowd of students in the Administration glass-house. They would have listened. He could have climbed on a computer-desk and said it to them. He would have got his audience. They would have been enthralled when he described how Gorlston had tried to blackmail him into smearing Berkeley. But that did not mean they would do anything about it. Given the idea that Berkeley was a Yellow, they were liable to think that Gorlston had behaved in a natural way.

I don't get it, Len thought as he went out of the glass portal and stood looking in both directions across the blue grass of the campus.

Maybe other people were more sophisticated than he was. He had been caught before by the way Arcon people were liable to talk about justice and free speech and democracy and similar ideals, and then, when something happened to make nonsense of their protestations, to go on in the same way but with a more cynical outlook. After being caught out on a limb, Len had come to the conclusion that they were all half-baked.

He could not see anyone keeping an eye on him on the campus, so he slipped away, not toward the students' block where he was supposed to go, but toward the public streets.

It was not easy to know where to go, as soon as he had done that and was on the run from the Information Office. He was going to need help and friends, and if possible contact with the revolutionary forces of Arcon. If any. He kept his eyes open for men in gray suits and tried not to hurry too much as he made his way to the monorail stop where he could get transport to downtown Davis City. As far as he could see, he had not been followed from the college.

Downtown was the less well-to-do part of Davis City where his parents had lived before they died. Len did not know of any actual revolutionary forces there, but at least in theory it was where they ought to be. To get there was the first hurdle. At the monorail station, a man in a gray suit made a cross connection and got on the car in front of him. Len waited for the next train.

There was no law that Information Office men had to wear gray suits. They usually did. But a man in a gray suit was not necessarily an Information Officer. It was difficult.

Len was a little doubtful as the journey progressed. He left the broad campus and highly individual and expensive buildings of the better part of Davis City, and, as he saw the harborfront shacks and warehouses along the swampglades ahead, he wondered whether he was altogether wise to seek that part of the city. It was not that he did not know it, but much of what he thought was college theory.

The people in downtown Davis City lived mostly in shacks among the steaming creeks and, in theory, as Len knew, they owned nothing, and had nothing to sell except their daughters, and nothing to hire out except their bodies, provided, that was, that the bodies were sufficiently healthy to be worth hiring. In theory, Len knew, these were the people who ought to respond to a cry of "Workers of Arcon arise, you have nothing to lose but your chains." It was just that Len was skeptical. He had to tell himself that when men had landed on Arcon they had all been free and equal, but now everything was owned by someone, while a lot of people owned nothing and did not seem to be able to get anything, either.

He got off the monorail car in the waterfront area and looked about him. The first thing he saw was an open tavern with sprawled drunks, spilled glasses, and broken furniture. For a moment he stopped and looked at it and thought that maybe it was not so much that a revolution was not needed on Arcon, as that the people who needed it did not seem capable of carrying it out—which was bad luck for him.

But he remembered his parents, who had been poor and sick but not drunk, and thought maybe what the people needed was help. College education was not necessarily an advantage, but he might try to give it.

He went on past a warehouse of a hover-barge transportation company, and along the quay above the ripesmelling mud of the hover-barge inlet, until he came to a shack proclaiming its one-room office and weatherboard to be the headquarters of the Davis City Downtown Dockers Union, C-branch. He knocked on the door and, since that produced no answer, he pushed it open and went in. "Hello, Joe," he said to the man who was waking up inside.

The man, who was aged forty, which meant he was shortly going to die in the Arcon way, looked at him sourly. "Why, Len," he said. "You left that college and got a good job yet? You come to give your father's old mates a handout?"

What Len did not know, among the many things that any young man of Len's age did not know on Arcon, was that he had been followed all the way in the course of his journey across Davis City. An unobtrusive man in a gray suit had been reading a newspaper in the far back corner of the monorail car, and while he was not the same man in a gray suit who had been passing the take-up point at just the time the train passed, he had nonetheless followed Len at a little distance. He was not in the least put out by the one-room shack. He looked at the sign on it, pulled a fine-printed book from his pocket and turned the pages, then, when he had found what he wanted, he behaved as though he knew the place, for he went around the back to listen.

Sure enough, around the back of the shack, there was a convenient place where a man could look as though he were doing nothing, or stand up against the wall, and hear everything that went on inside through a crack in ill-fitting boards. It was not that the Information Office lacked technical know-how. It was just that their operatives were told to be reasonable, and not go around putting microphones where none were needed.

Inside, Len said, "I am in trouble," and watched the old man called Joe cast a rheumy, swamp-fever eye at him.

Joe looked at him thoughtfully for a moment. "You take my advice," he said. "You tell the girl to look after it herself. It's her look-out."

"Not that kind of trouble," Len said after thought. "Political trouble."

Since there had not seemed to be a great deal of point in making his speech to the drunks and layabouts in the cafés along the waterfront, Len made it to Joe.

"I've been finding out things at college," he said. "It seems to me that I've been living my life in a state of illusion until just recently, Joe. Do you really think that this planet of ours was founded by a group of refugees who were escaping from something dreadful on Earth lest worse befall them? I've come to doubt it. Our ancestors may have left Earth in a state of nobility, for high ideals. I don't know what has gone wrong, but something has. I don't know if it's the Information Office or the Greens and Blues who are engaged in some sort of racket, but someone is. Who are the Yellow Party, and where are they? I need to know because I believe I've been declared a Yellow myself, and I'm going to be arrested."

Joe listened. There was that about Joe. He had lived as long as anyone could on Arcon, and he would not have held his position as union branch secretary except that he was capable of listening.

24

He did not reply about the Yellow Party.

"I don't know about high ideals," Joe said. "But I've thought that myself about the Information Office and the political parties for years and years. Why, Len, for a dewy-eyed lad, you're almost politically conscious."

Len was disappointed that his revelations, and particularly the one that he was going to be arrested, and therefore surely ought to be taken seriously, did not have more effect on Joe.

"You've known them? But look, Joe, if you've known what I know, why haven't you been arrested?"

Len did not know how things worked on Arcon.

"I haven't had a college education," Joe said. "I'm not supposed to be articulate." Joe looked back on a wasted life. "Furthermore, I've never tried to rock the boat; haven't you noticed that? You tell me how to get my dockers an extra three centicredits an hour, and that's all they and I want."

Len looked at Joe in a baffled way. In truth, he was having second thoughts now about the wisdom of having come to Joe. He might have known, he thought, just to look at the swampcreeks and downtown Davis City, that nothing of any wisdom or strength of purpose could ever come out of that. He began to march up and down Joe's shack.

"We should rebel," he said. "We should speak out fearlessly and tell the people all the truth. We should eliminate corruption in high places, and expose the political parties. Maybe we should take to arms, and strike down those who oppose us with our own right hands. Men should be comrades. They should be brothers to one another. We must have a program. We must subvert the police, and then the army. We must foment unrest, and bring your dockers out on strike immediately. But first we must arrange for my own safety. I shall have to arrange to stow away on a hover-barge. Can you fix that, Joe?"

Outside the shack, the man in the gray suit shook a small tape-recorder he had been holding up against the crack in the shack-wall. He looked at it critically and noted the time in his notebook, then marked the tape. It was enough, he thought. When they started preaching revolution, it was quite enough. You did not want to overdo it. He came around to the front door.

"I'm damned if I'm going to involve my dockers in some kind of college-student spree," Joe said. "I'm due to get my pension if I can live for another three months, and believe me, I'm going to get it."

The man in the gray suit came in.

"All right, Joe," he said. "Just stand back a little. It won't do you any good at all to get in this spray-gun's line."

Len was looking at the man in the gray suit, and at the object, the last item in an Information Office agent's equipment, which the man was holding. Len went mad at that point. He could not claim afterward that he acted unthinkingly, or that he was surprised or shocked to find himself arrested. He took quite a long look at the man in the gray suit and then decided to rush him.

He was lying in a cell when he woke up.

A man he knew as Berkeley, a college history lecturer, was bending over him.

VII

From *The Arcon Records*:

Arcon lived by a balance of power.

No planet at that time lived as it did because of external forces. No impulsion from outside said a government had to be this or that. No compulsion said a government had to retain its form for five hundred years. Arcon was kept as it was by internal pressures.

Or maybe by the army.

The army was created before the Information Office. The army dated right back to the time when separate settlements were set up on Arcon. The army was not meant to fight anyone. It was said, even at the time of the founding of the fighting army, that it was there to keep the peace. Communications had proved unusually difficult on the apparently innocent planet, and the army ran them.

So none of the separate settlements on Arcon became separate nations. Arcon remained a unified single-government planet, and that was the army.

Since there was the army, it was hard to see, from the army point of view, why the Information Office should exist at all. The Information Office quietly dealt with internal, and especially urban security, and arrested Yellows.

There was no unified command including both army and Information Office. Command was a matter of informing the government, or individuals within the government, and doing this or that. From the government, funds flowed downward, both ways. And the fact that the funds might flow more one way and less the other was one cause of the internal pressures.

A man called Davis, a descendent of the William Davis who founded Davis City, was crude about it. He said, "If what the government chooses to spend on security is a cake, then the chief aim in life of the Information Office and the army, and the substance of the reports each puts in to the government, is that it should get its slice, its share."

William Davis' descendent was unpopular. He died by falling out of a window, but no one knew quite how. But the balance of power on Arcon remained intact, and maybe, if the politicians kept both an army and an Information Office, it was to play the one against the other.

Such a stasis was always subject to little tremors.

On October 25, 502 A.L., such a tremor happened. It took the form of an interview, four years before the events that were to result from it, in the office of Commandant C. Q. Lankowitz, in the large but not conspicuous Information Office building of Davis City.

The Commandant had commanded the Information Office H.Q. and Capital Division for a few months by then. He was a spare, academic man, at an electronic desk, and the special occasion was what might be regarded as a courtesy call on him by a General J. Koln, newly appointed to the command of the Arcon First Army, also based in the capital area.

It was natural that the two men, who were strangers, should talk mostly in terms of civilities for a little time. Each knew that the other was a power in the land. The post of Commandant of the Information Office in the capital area was more than just a local command, and the General, sitting comfortably in the visitor's chair across the desk from the Commandant, had a perfectly good office of his own in a building called the Hexagon, not many miles away.

"Since we are both relatively new to our posts," the General said, looking around at the interior of an Information Office with interest, "it seemed to me reasonable to call on you to express the hope that we might avoid the friction that has characterized the relations between our offices in the past."

What the General was looking around for was not very clear. It might have been hidden microphones.

"It was indeed unfortunate," the Commandant said, "that your predecessor should have developed such a strong feeling that the Information Office had something to do with

27

the Treasury insistence on cutting down on the army estimates."

The two men looked at one another across the desk and understood one another.

The General said abruptly, with another glance at the walls and window of the room, "Can we talk in here?"

The Commandant raised his eyebrows at the suggestion that anyone, no matter who he was, might not feel free to talk as he pleased in an Information Office.

"I mean talk," the General said. "In your own interest what I have to say may not be something you would want on a public record."

The Commandant reached across the desk and pushed a switch to OFF. Naturally he did not tell the General that the switch only switched the system of recording from a relatively open to a more private kind.

The Commandant himself spoke more freely when that was done. "General," he said, "let's face it." He looked at his visitor more narrowly. "Now that Arcon is a more urban civilization, and the Information Office has such control of the cities, the possibilities of revolt grow less and less. Do you want me to talk frankly?"

"Do," the General said.

"Then, since the Information Office now has such complete control, you must expect that the army estimates will go on being reduced. To put it bluntly, you should count yourself lucky that no one has yet suggested that the army should be disbanded."

The General went on sitting as he was, in an amicable way.

"Alternatively," he said, "since the Yellows are no longer a force on Arcon, it might be the Information Office that could be disbanded."

The Commandant shook his head. "Unlike the army, which has no visible opponent and no external enemy to Arcon in sight," he said. "We go on arresting Yellows every day."

"You are sure they are Yellows?" the General said. "And not just your political opponents?"

The Commandant looked again at the General, who was looking far more self-confident than he had a right to be.

"That is a treasonable suggestion."

"I agree," the General said with care and thought, "that it would be convenient if the army *did* have an external enemy against whom it could defend our state of Arcon."

28

The Commandant looked at the General most carefully, wondering exactly what he was suggesting.

The General withdrew a paper from the briefcase he had brought with him. "My predecessor," he said, "expanded his military intelligence units."

"There is absolutely no need for that," the Commandant said. "It is against government policy. Information and intelligence is strictly the province of the Information Office."

The General went on fingering the paper he had taken from his briefcase.

"The Information Office has made such a good business out of catching Yellows that the army thought it would try too," he said. "It was quite an interesting exercise. We had some of our men set up in civilian clothes, and aim to be captured by your Information Office, and other things."

For some reason, the Commandant did not respond at once. He ran his tongue across his lips and went on looking at the sheaf of papers in the General's hands.

The General watched him.

"How is your internal security, Commandant?" he asked. "Have you ever thought, in the political climate of Arcon, and in view of there being nowhere else that was safe for them to go, there might be some Yellows actually *inside* the Information Office?"

The suggestion that the General had just made, as everyone knew, was perfectly preposterous.

The Information Office, that security arm of the Arcon administration, was employed specifically to counter and check and crush the Yellows. It arrested them every day. It interfered with people's lives. It had people rejected when they applied for the highest jobs, on "security" grounds, and because they were not "safe" characters. The Information Office, on one or two notable occasions, had even been known to indict and accuse the highest politicians, who had later been removed from office.

Yet there was the General, saying that there might be Yellows actually *inside* the Information Office, and there was the Commandant, not saying anything, but sitting with an air of caution, and a little rigidly, and looking at the paper in the General's hands.

The General passed across the paper. "It's only a copy, of course," were the words with which he accompanied it. Then, as though his courtesy call was over, he got up to leave the Commandant.

He paused on the way out, and turned back to the desk again.

"You have heard about the cake?" he said.

"Cake?"

He looked hard at the Commandant. "The cake of which our organizations both get slices."

"Yes." After a moment, there was something almost luminous about the way the Commandant looked at the General, as though he understood him right down from what was inside his head to what was inside his trousers.

"The solution to the problem of larger slices may be to obtain a larger cake." The General, perhaps intentionally, looked upward at the ceiling. "It would be useful if Arcon had an external enemy," he said.

The Commandant's gaze relaxed and became mild as the General's eyes came down. He looked once again like someone who thought academically in terms of policies, Blue government, the chances of the Greens at the next election, the administration of a busy office, and kindred matters. He no longer appeared to notice the over-heavy innocence of the man before him.

"Your suggestion will be attended to, General, and it is certainly of interest to us that we might avoid the friction."

The General went out, looking aggressive and pleased with himself, and Commandant C. Q. Lankowitz sat at his desk and thought for a while, with narrowed eyes.

VIII

From *the diary of J. Adolf Koln:*

July 9, 502 A.L.

Since I have come into the capital, I have learned that I must make contacts with my opposite numbers in the Information Office. In a way, they are at once the colleagues and the competitors of the army, since they too are concerned with the security of the planet, but in some instances it is either them or us. This is a game played in kid gloves, and I am not used to it.

July 13, 502 A.L.

Something has happened. I have heard an atrocious story. It is too scandalous to be confided to this journal.

July 25, 502 A.L.

I have always thought the Information Office to be genuine. Even now I cannot believe otherwise. Yet

*what am I to think? I cannot believe that men can
exist as they are, if what I have heard is true.*

July 29, 502 A.L.
*I feel I am reaching some kind of crisis. There is some-
thing abominable about going about the capital and
hearing the scandal and all the gossip. Some of the politicians think that I know more than I already do, I think.
Do they not understand that I would not behave as I
do if I believed even a fraction of what I heard? It is
their assumption that I am like them that leaves me de-
filed, and I am sick with the treachery of it.*

August 1, 502 A.L.
*I have solved the problem of my oath. It is true that
this oath, required of all who hold a commission in the
Arcon Army, pledges allegiance to the rightful government of Arcon, but this I am sure is purely nominal,
and inserted by the politicians, while the true meaning
is something deeper. My loyalty, I am convinced, is not
to a group of politicians who are most unworthy. It is
to the Arcon people.*

IX

From the *Information Office Headquarters File:*

*Office of the
District Captain,
Anti-Yellow Division,
Capital Area.
July 30, 205 A.L.*

*The Commandant,
Anti-Yellow Division.*

Dear Commandant Lankowitz,
*It is naturally with some reserve that, at your request,
I made a character report on G. Berkeley, my own sec-
ond-in-command in this district. Though I appreciate
your remarks on my laxity, I still feel it is invidious for a
captain to report on subordinates only one step down in
our internal hierarchy.*
*There is absolutely no doubt about the intelligence,
enthusiasm and ability of Lieutenant G. Berkeley. My
reservations relate rather to his romanticism and idealism,
which, excellent as they are, make me feel that they*

*may preclude him from higher office. It is very difficult
to pin this down. A tendency to don disguises and do
things himself when he feels they should be done well,
instead of delegating work to others, is typical. I do
not know why I feel that this man would be unreliable
in higher office, but I do.*

Respectfully yours,

M. Pilsen (Captain, Capital Area)

X

UNDERSTANDING, while knowing nothing.

Leaping to conclusions, even if they were the wrong ones.
They were bound to be wrong, anyway. It was not a
very good cell, but, to begin with, Len had only a hazy
impression of it.

"All right, ease up, Len," Berkeley said. "Try uncurling
your limbs a little. It's painful, I know, but you really
shouldn't try to rush a spray-gun."

The man and the voice were known, but not the sense
the things the voice said. The cell was ten feet by six,
with toilet and white tiles, which made it look quite clean.
The way it looked so uninviting could be the pain.

"Where am I?" Len tried to say. "What happened?"

Make sense of things if he could. He couldn't.

Berkeley did not try to answer two questions simultaneously, since Len's speech was not back to normal yet.

"You're in I.O. headquarters," he said in his new way.
"Maybe I should say under I.O. headquarters. This cell, if
I remember the way I came down here, is about three
levels underground."

It was another feature of the cell. It had a light, but
no window. Len became conscious of that. Instead of trying to stand up and do something, he concentrated on being conscious.

"Mr. Berkeley," he said.

"Well, um, yes," Berkeley said. "Mr. Berkeley."

Len opened his eyes wide. He even succeeded in sitting up a little. Perhaps it was not wise, but he stuck with
it. He looked around him.

"Mr. Berkeley," Len said. "Why, they've put me in the
same cell with you."

Berkeley looked as though he would like to answer that,
but he desisted. He seemed to think it was too complicated.
He took a packet out of his pocket and handed Len an
Arcon cigarette. Smoking was not wise on Arcon. It short-

ened your life by five years, and out of forty that was quite a proportion, but there were times when it was worth it.

"Take it easy," he said.

Len repeated his former question. "What happened?"

"You've been tested," Berkeley said.

"Tested?" Len thought he meant arrested.

"You tried to change the world around you," Berkeley said. "It wasn't a very good attempt. I was a bit disappointed about that. Still, you did it, and since I forecast it, I'm glad to have been right about that."

Len took another look at the cell and Berkeley. There was something that was not quite right, even in wrongness.

It was a cell, all right, and it was underground, but the door was open. Berkeley had a bath-sponge in his hand, which he had used to bathe Len's face to bring him around, but since it was unlikely that prisoners were provided with bath-sponges in their cells, Berkeley must have got it from down the corridor. Also, Berkeley was wearing a gray suit.

It was quite a high-class gray suit. It was a better gray suit than Gorlston had worn, and it was a far better gray suit than the somewhat baggy and crushed one that the man who had come into the shack had been wearing, though Len had only seen him momentarily, and had not been precisely interested in his clothes. All the same, it was a gray suit.

"Mr. Berkeley," Len said. "I somehow don't think I've got this quite right."

"I'm fairly sure you haven't," Berkeley said. "Oh, well, we all make mistakes at times."

Len looked at the open door, and then at Berkeley. "I suppose you are a prisoner here?" he said.

"No," Berkeley said. "Not exactly. No. It's not quite fair to put it like that. You might say that I am the opposite."

Len took a little time thinking about the pins and needles which afflicted all his limbs, and also about what Berkeley could mean about being the opposite of a prisoner in the particular context in which he used it.

"You are in the hands of the authorities," Berkeley said encouragingly. "To be precise, and to put a finer point on it, if you think you can take it, me."

"I don't get this," Len said.

Berkeley sighed. "I didn't think you would."

But he dropped the sponge with some distaste, and seemed to think that Len was all right now, for he sat down on the bunk opposite him and made himself comfortable, as though he was going to stay for a little time.

"Have I been arrested?" Len said.

"You can put it that way. You can say you are under restraint. It will sound a little better."

"You mean I am a prisoner here?" Len looked at the open door. "And you are not?"

"It will take too long to get at it the question and answer way," Berkeley said. "Let's have it out, shall we? You are my prisoner. I gave orders to Gorlston, and then to have you followed, and then, when you became violent, which I anticipated, to have you arrested."

It took Len a little time to think out what Berkeley had told him. For some reason it seemed to him particularly fateful and underhanded. After all, he had got into his present state in part because of Berkeley. He had defended Berkeley as far as he could against Gorlston, and then, when it came to the crunch, he had also been thinking of Berkeley when he had resisted being blackmailed into a smear.

For a very ordinary student, with a pronounced but reasonably harmless aptitude for mathematics and electronics, fate seemed to be unusually unkind.

"The world and our Arcon politics are the way I thought they were," Len said. "Things aren't less bad then I thought. They're more so."

"I assume you are being philosophical," Berkeley said. "Our planet is in a bad way. It always has been. I'll agree to that." He added, "I'm a ranking I. O. officer."

"Why?" Len said. "Why, why, why?"

"It's the payoff balance," Berkeley said. "It might have been studied in any society. It could have been. But there's been no cause before."

Len realized, with difficulty, that Berkeley was talking about the State of Arcon. It was not exactly the question Len had asked. What he had meant to ask was why Berkeley had appeared at his college as a pseudo history lecturer, misled him, attracted him with fine words, befriended him, deserted him, got him into trouble with Gorlston, had him followed, then had him knocked out with a spray-gun, and finally had him arrested and thrown into prison.

It did not seem a logical procedure to Len. He could not make out why anyone should do it, regardless of who Berkeley was. But he was still remembering his state of mind just before he got knocked out with the spray-gun, and he saw even less cause to change it now than he had then. He decided to play it Berkeley's way.

"I know we had some interesting sociological discussions in the past, Mr. Berkeley, but do you mind explaining to me, among other things, what you mean by the 'payoff balance'? I don't think I've heard that term before."

Berkeley looked very serious.

"The payoff balance," he said, "is the difference between the length of a man's useful working life, which obviously depends on how long he lives to work, and the length of the period of education which is necessary to fit him for that work. This may seem very difficult and abstract and irrelevant to you, Len. But for the past four hundred and fifty years, it has dictated virtually everything that has happened here on Arcon."

Len also looked serious. "Including what has happened to me?" he said.

"It's like this," Berkeley said. "Our ancestors, when they arrived here on Arcon, didn't know anything about the payoff balance. You wouldn't expect them to, would you? It had not been studied. And besides, being farmers and constructional engineers, and pioneers generally, they were only concerned with two things. One was how they could live, which they did fairly well, having a virtually virgin planet to exploit, and the other was the awful and incomprehensible fact that they died at forty. You probably don't understand the significance of that last fact, Len. You're used to it, and were brought up with it, the idea that forty is the natural dying age for people. To our ancestors, though, it loomed as the largest and most incomprehensible fact in all their lives. What science and time they could spare, under the leadership of the Greens, was devoted to biochemistry, when they could afford biochemistry, and the attempt to solve the problem."

"I'm not sure I altogether follow this," Len said. "I find it difficult at the moment to concentrate my mind on what happened four hundred and fifty years ago. I'm thinking more of now."

What a way to begin an education.

"Four hundred years ago," Berkeley said. "Three hundred years ago. It amounts to the same thing. You see—and I'm sorry to have to acquaint you with this, Len—the problem is insoluble. Even now, after four hundred years of research, we still don't know how the human Earth-born metabolism of man can be reconciled with the biochemistry of Arcon. I can tell you how much we do know. We know that the problem arises because there are different characteristic compounds in the biological organisms in Arcon

35

air and Arcon dust and water. It's a bit more difficult than growing an acid-soil plant in a chalk and lime soil. And while you may think it should be easy for a chemist, the answer is that it would be if only one substance was involved or some simple thing. If it was just the water, for instance, then we could distill the water. Or if it was just the air, then we could wear face-masks. But unfortunately these compounds are not only in the air and water, but they are a natural part of the soil and the things we eat. It isn't practicable to grow everything under artificial conditions, and if we did all the plants and beef would have to be given distilled water and be put in helmets too. It's complicated, as you can see, and the fact remains that the only way man could have lived fully on Arcon, to his natural three-score-years-and-ten, would have been to stay in a self-sustaining system, which is to say inside the spaceship."

Len was shocked by Berkeley's description of the situation on Arcon, his home planet.

None of the books he had ever read, which dealt with the logistics of getting to new star-systems and other worlds, had told him anything about the true chemical and biochemical problems that man might encounter once he got there, and that his ancestors had encountered and put up with. He did not want to think of it.

"Mr. Berkeley, what's this got to do with the other thing you mentioned?" he said. "The whatever-it-was, the pay-off balance?"

"The connection is this, Len: Our forefathers, for five hundred years, have tried to solve the problem of making people on Arcon live longer than forty, and they have failed. So, naturally, they've thought from time to time in other terms. In Yellow Party terms, for example. If the only way to enable people to live a natural, full and lengthy life on Arcon would be to keep them in a spaceship, then why not put everyone in spaceships? Go off to another planet, in other words. But that is where our people have run up against a difficulty. After the original spaceship had been destroyed, it proved not so easy to put it together again or make a new one. And to make a whole fleet of starships, which was what would have been necessary after two or three generations, was quite beyond our powers. A very high technological civilization would be necessary to do a thing like that. And a very high technological civilization means that people have to have a lengthy education. Do you know that on Earth, the people who built the great technological civilization there were all educated beyond the age of thirty? But of what use would it be to us, on Arcon, to educate our people, students like you, to the age of thirty-plus, which is what we'd have to do to make a civilization capable of building a fleet of starships, when you'll all be dead by forty? If you think carefully of this for a little, you'll see what I mean by the payoff balance."

Len did. Awkward and acute as his own position was, with a highly uncertain future, a prisoner in a cell, guarded by Berkeley, for the first time he saw something of the awful dilemma that surrounded all life on Arcon.

He even found time to be sorry not only for himself, but for everyone else, and the people of Arcon as a whole. It made it worse that he had not previously realized that there was a problem, far less such an intractable, obscure, but fatal one.

"You mean that in order to solve Arcon's problems, or build a fleet of starships, we'd have to educate everyone to thirty-five?"

"Not everyone, Len. No civilization requires that all its people should be educated to quite the same age. It might do if we could educate the vast majority of the people to your age, say around twenty-two. Only a few would have to go on studying, and gaining experience, to thirty-five or forty. But that's one of the troubles we've always had on Arcon. We've never had men who've been both well educated *and* experienced as administrators. All our early disasters on the planet, the ones that were blamed on Yellow sabotage, were due to that. We did fine as long as we were a low-grade farming community. It was when we began to try to run airlines, expand the power program and industrialize, that we found that people who had stopped learning at twenty, and since then had done things by guesswork and rule of thumb, weren't up to it. Our administrators, appointed at thirty-five to jobs that on Earth would have been done by a man of sixty, were either ill-educated, or they were fully educated but inexperienced, reckless. That is the payoff balance law. A very primitive farming community can exist even if the average age at death is twenty-five, as it was in some places on Earth at one time. To be industrialized to the point we're at on Arcon requires a life-expectancy of at least forty years. But to be industrialized on the interplanetary and starship scale needs something more than we can achieve on Arcon, and so we're stuck."

Len looked at Berkeley, then shook his head to clear his brain, and then met Berkeley's eyes.

"So the Yellows were right," he said. "Far from this planet proving a piece of cake, as the Greens thought, or from man adapting to it as the Blues said, it's proved a trap, and we can neither progress while on this planet, nor get off it."

"That's true, Len," Berkeley replied a little thoughtfully. "Though of course we can't admit it. You know how it is. People like you may understand these things, if they are put to you and someone takes the trouble to go to considerable length about it, but it isn't nice knowledge, and that's one of the jobs of the Information Office: to keep it secret and ban the Yellows so they can't go around saying 'I told you so,' and stirring up the common people."

"So that the Greens and Blues can keep their power," Len said. "So that they won't have any trouble with inconvenient things like facts, and can continue to rule and perpetuate their mistakes forever."

"Be reasonable, Len," Berkeley said. "You can see it isn't like that. What good would it have done, after we were here, if the Greens and Blues had said, 'Sorry, the situation's hopeless; we were wrong and made a mistake, and this planet is a trap'? We'd never have built a civilization that way, or got as far as we have. There's a lot to be said for the Greens and Blues. They didn't give up when they saw their mistake. It was for the public good that they took steps to prevent the truth from coming out, and they acted like responsible people in relation to their mistake, and stayed right in there battling."

Sitting up on his bunk, Len thought that Berkeley's defense of the Greens and Blues, ingenious as it was, might well be used to excuse anyone covering up after any mistake at all. With his eye, he measured the distance between Berkeley and the door, and wondered if he could make a dash for it. The pain in his limbs was less, and he thought he could run now. But he remembered that Berkeley had said they were three floors down, and he could hardly expect to get out without meeting any guards at all, and to be laid out twice by a spray-gun charge within twenty-four hours might well be fatal.

"So why am I here?" he said, keeping talking.

"So I can tell you all this," Berkeley said, raising his eyebrows as though it should be obvious. "In prison and under firm security is obviously the place to do it. Especially as the idea is that you don't come out again unless you accept a suggestion I am going to put to you. I have news for you, Len. I am authorized to put it to you on behalf of the government and the security agencies. Len, we have a job for you."

XI

The Shopping Lists of Mary Jean Smith:

> Nightdresses 2
> Bras 3
> The blue dress or the green.
> Panties ?   (!)

> Wedding gown fitting is at 2:30.

> When phoning John, say I do hope
> he knows what he's doing, poor dear
> (but don't say it too much).

XII

From *The Jottings of G. Berkeley*:

Everyone can see me outside, but what am I like inside? Maybe these jottings will help me to know this.

I am a citizen of Davis City. By this I mean that I am not actually ambitious or mercenary. It is just that because I was born among the vertical blocks of the concrete waste of the capital, I behave as the city does. Our city authorities had no need to build upward either. We could have expanded into the desert. But because we are the planet's first city we have a kind of style, and we build these towers and flyovers and parks and surely far-too-ostentatious bridges across the creeks. We don't care if we impress the provincials, and are far too cynical to think we impress ourselves, so it must be one another.

I don't know what good it will do to keep these jottings. As far as my progress in the Information Office goes, I look back on a wasted year. I have gone to the office in the morning and come back in the evening. Occasionally, though less often than I had to in the past, I have gone to some part of the city to interview some poor fool who has trembled at the thought that the Information Office is taking an interest in him. It is true that Pilsen is failing, but who likes to wait for dead men's shoes?

Most people in the city measure their progress in life by their personal relationships with one another. Who is an I.O. officer of my rank supposed to have a relationship with? It can hardly be his "clients"; his subordinates are out of the question, and attempts to be friendly with his superiors would look like currying favor. There's a young man I have dealings with . . . It is better to confine myself to the office. I can't help but see that Captain Pilsen, who hates me, is failing fast. His work in the office is often not done, unless it is done by me, and even his grip on security is relaxing, and I think the Commandant knows it. I hate to think of these things.

Now that there is a chance, if only a chance, that I may be appointed to Pilsen's job, it is time I stopped thinking about office politics and thought more of grand strategy and general policy, for which I have a taste. I must try to feel again the wonder I first felt when I heard that the Yellows have a controlling interest in the Information Office, the very organization that is supposed to be engaged in suppressing Yellows.

It is a matter of history, but I still get troubled when I think of the subject with all its ironic turns and twists, which are political fortune. Two hundred years ago there was not the slightest chance that we could become almost part of the government, secure, salaried, and part of an organization whose every doing is cloaked with the magic word "security." We were a tiny minority then, persecuted and defeated, outlawed and losing our members fast. Everyone had to suffer during the period of Great Disaster that hit our planet, but we had to endure the hatred of the people too. It was not only that people struggling for existence were sick of space adventures and Yellow Doctrines, but the Green and Blue parties had just put out the fatal smear, blaming us for their own mistakes by saying we were causing the disasters by our sabotage. How disastrous all this was. It should have finished us. Yet how ironic.

I wonder sometimes how many other governments in the course of human history have made the same mistake? It must look so logical and attractive to many rulers, to set up an information office to defeat the opposition and act as a secret police above the law. Especially since the opposition was helpless; they could not go wrong.

There is a kind of grim inevitability about it. It has been seen countless times in history. How can the politicians not see that they have to become the prisoners and tools of the organization that supplies them with the information on which they act—an organization which they themselves have allowed to cloak its doing with that magic and fatal word "security"? There has never been a government yet, whether a dictatorship or a so-called nominal democracy, that, having set up an organization of our kind, has not found its actions guided, ultimately, into the most appalling mistakes, or into paths of action that have nothing to do with its own aims, but everything to do with the interests of the organization which it has itself created. The politicians themselves lose the power to check their information as they get it. The propaganda services, which are supposed to serve them, are used to fix the very elections by which the politicians attain their office. "Whoever runs the I.O. rules the world," we say—except that he never needs to get elected, and the way he achieves his power is by a political struggle that is completely hidden.

It was that genius T. L. Lankowitz, ancestor of our present C. Q. Lankowitz, who first saw this, and who advanced thought on Arcon in the one branch it has excelled in, which is social science. One of the aims of my ambition in our office is to rise high enough in the hierarchy to be able to talk with C. Q. on equal terms and ask him what his ancestor was really like. We were utterly defeated and unpopular, I remember. The I. O. did not exist. The Disasters were happening and driving people out of the cities again and back to rural life, and in the climate of those times anyone expressing a Yellow opinion was tarred and feathered by a spontaneous outburst of the people against thought of any kind. It was then that T. L. Lankowitz, after presiding over the dismayed rump of our 289th Council, sent his communication to the Blue and Green leaders who formed the National Coalition government: "Defeated, and wishing to save our lives and those of our families, we are willing to admit our errors . . . prepared, in return for mercy at a public trial, to confess that the great disasters have been caused by our sabotage." Then his courage in the dock, admitting to crimes it would have been impossible for us to have committed, yet somehow sounding convincing and more patriotic than the Blues and Greens!

It was his second stroke which showed his genius, his

realization of the inevitable progression of events. Already he had persuaded the government to set up the Information Office, moved, he said, by the fears of a renegade, that the Yellows who had smeared their party at the trial in return for mercy would be assassinated by the Yellows still at large. The Disasters still went on, which was public proof that there were Yellows still at large, and no one could deny that Lankowitz and his group had most need to fear them, and the life-or-death incentive to round them up. No one hated or feared a revolutionary party more than a renegade who had left it, and so he moved himself and his group into a wing of the Information Office. It was hidden then, the ruthlessness with which he used his powers to kill off, arrest or accuse all the key men who opposed him, and so take control from inside. From defeat to power. Surely this is the most beautiful example of the genius of a man's brain.

Those days are past now, and we have moderated from our revolutionary fervor, but the thing I still admire about our organization is its expertise. High ideals are all very well, and indeed I have them, but what people everywhere admire most are the men who know what they are doing and get things done, like us, the true professionals.

XIII

RELIEVED AS Len was to be offered a way out by taking a job, he was sure that if the work was attractive, Berkeley would not have found it necessary to put him in a cell before he offered it. It was good to have information, but it was also possible to pay a too-heavy price for it.

"Since I have come to the end of my college career, I think you can take it that I am looking for a job of some kind."

"You'll take it, then?"

"I think you might tell me what it is first."

"It isn't that kind of job, Len. It's a kind you'll have to pick up and learn about as you go along."

Len looked at Berkeley and wondered if there was any alternative. Staying in the cell, he imagined. It was not exactly a choice to give him enthusiasm for his new work. He sat on the edge of his bunk, pondering.

"It's a privilege to be offered this job, Len," Berkeley said. "I won't pretend there aren't some risks attached to it, but just think for a moment of the trouble I've gone to in selecting you."

Len had thought of it, and was not sure he liked it. What he felt was that he would have some freedom of action if he accepted Berkeley's offer, and none if he stayed in the cell. He stood up.

"I'll take it."

Berkeley looked hard at him for a moment. He was not very convinced of Len's sincerity, but did not make a point of it. There was momentarily something in Berkeley's look that was like regret, as though he was thinking of something that might-have-been. But he was practical about Len's acceptance, and motioned him to the door, looking at his watch as if keeping an expected schedule.

Len thought about aims and objectives as he preceded Berkeley out of the cell. In a way, he trusted Berkeley. He had been truthful when he had told Gorlston that on the whole he thought that Berkeley was, or could be, a good man. But he did not trust him too far. Life on Arcon, he thought as he went along the corridor and discovered that his cell was one of a row of cells, was not like that. He looked about him and discovered that the Information Office cells were surprisingly clean and antiseptic and efficient, with no signs of the torture he had once heard went on there, but they were nonetheless cells, and a place for secret incarceration under a considerable building, for all that.

He saw that he had been right in thinking that it would have been no good to beat Berkeley to the door and make a dash down the corridor. The whole thing was run on careful and evidently long-established lines that the people in the streets above could not suspect. "You want him out, Captain?" the guard at the end of the corridor said, and unlocked a gate that let them through to an elevator, where another man in uniform looked carefully at Berkeley before he took them to a higher floor.

I am going to be careful before I step out of line again on Arcon, Len thought. Then he found reason to doubt whether he would ever have the chance to step out of line again on Arcon. They emerged by a small room and a side door onto the ground floor and were stopped again at a barrier before they could reach the more public part. Pretty secretaries, men in gray suits, and some members of the public could be seen there, going about what looked like their ordinary but somewhat worrying business, in their normal way.

"You'll have to sign for him, and I'm afraid you ought to take an escort, Captain," a man at an office window said.

"He can't get out of my car on the expressway."

"There's always the other end, sir."

"He'll be well taken care of there."

Berkeley got his way, by rank, but had to sign a book and accept a personal responsibility for Len, and another armed guard was summoned to escort Len to Berkeley's car in the parking lot and see him securely inside with the door closed before they started.

As they maneuvered onto the rack accelerator and were shot out onto the freeway, Len wondered, in view of what had happened, what elaborate precautions there were going to be at the other end.

It felt strangely different for him to ride in the car in the curving concrete and metal track and look out on the city with the sensation of it being so near and yet so far. How many times had he walked in those streets down there, not doing anything in particular, as a free and youthful citizen? It was almost, he thought as they shot around the spiderframe of the business section, as though he would never do such a thing again. To be free and able to do nothing, he thought, looking at the crowds of busy people. They did not know how lucky they were. If they only exerted their freedom and stood still for a while, it might be the first step toward their doing anything.

"Where are we going?" he asked Berkeley.

"We'll take the next left turn if this vehicle goes the way I set up the dial."

It was not the way to the college. It led out into the desert, but although it was busy, with a constant train of vehicles whipping past on Len's side, it was not the way to the civil airport. There was only one other place they could go, heading out of town in that direction, and Len confirmed it by noticing the number of dun-colored vehicles on the track once they were past the intersection, and the number of uniforms inside them.

"I always wondered why we needed a standing army on Arcon," Len said. "Since we've never had a war that I have heard of."

Looking at a hexagonal-shaped building that was rising out of the flatlands ahead, on the fringe of the city where it met the desert, Berkeley said, "It has its uses." He did not deny that it was to the army headquarters that they were going.

Len tried to think of what kind of job he could be given that was connected with the army, but could think of nothing. As they went on approaching the building, he said to Berkeley, "Does this mean that I'm going to be conscripted?"

"No," said Berkeley. "Not exactly that."

Len could think of nothing to do with the army that was not formal and official. He tried to work out something that the army and the Information Office combined could use him for, and failed. But they were going to the Hexagon. When they reached the guard-point at the entrance to the grounds, which included an army airfield laid out in the desert at the back, Berkeley showed the guard a paper, and the soldier looked at the paper and at Len as though he had been expecting something of the kind, and been warned of it. "Closed section 203 E," he said, pointing.

As soon as the car had stopped a group of armed soldiers had surrounded it. Berkeley had been right that Len had no chance of leaping out and making a bolt for it.

They drove not toward, but around the side of the extensive building, passing another guard-point where a sergeant checked the number of the car before he raised a barrier, then closed it again behind them. They were in a small enclosed part of the airport area then, and Berkeley drove up to where a group of soldiers seemed to be waiting for them. Before they got out of the car, he touched Len, looked straight at him, and said, "Goodbye, Len. Remember you are Gorlston's and my selection, and try to live up to us, won't you?"

Len did not get the significance of that remark, except that Berkeley was talking as though he would not see him again.

"I think you might tell me what this is about," he said.

"You and the Chief of Staff?" said Berkeley. He looked at Len for a moment. "You've been picked," he said. Then he got out of the car.

He was right about what would happen when they got out. A sergeant waved Berkeley into an office, and a soldier jerked a thumb to Len and said, "This way, you," and set off with him while a squad of men fell in behind them. It was more the treatment given to a prisoner than a recruit or someone who was to do a job, Len thought. Berkeley had disappeared and they were heading toward the airfield.

The soldiers took Len to an isolated and guarded waiting room not far from the planes. Len did not ask them what it was all about because he guessed that they, unlike Berkeley, would not even know. A young man was being brought from the planes toward the waiting room at the same time Len got there. Inside, there was a surprise. Besides three young men already waiting there, there were five girls.

Len stood in the doorway looking at them. They looked like student types like himself, and when the door opened to let him in, they looked up as though they were expecting something to happen, though they did not know what. He only had to look at them to know in advance that they knew about as much as he did.

So this is not something that has happened just to me, Len thought, and he stood aside to let the new young man come in; he entered and looked around the room as though expecting to see someone there who could tell him something. "What is this?" the new young man said to everyone.

Whatever it was, both the army and the Information Office were involved in it, Len thought, and it was not a small thing, since it was being handled directly through the army headquarters at the Hexagon. Including himself there were twelve disgruntled young people altogether after another girl and a young man had come in from the planes and asked the same question, and he wondered if he ought to feel better or worse about it. What worried him was the memory of the somewhat doubtful and equivocal way that Berkeley had said goodbye to him.

XIV

From the Yellow Party archives:

Documents normally housed in a vault under the Information Office Emergency H. Q. at Parker's Knoll outside Davis City.

Minutes of a meeting of the Yellow Party Security Council held in the Information Office secrecy-annex on November 1, 502 A. L.

Agenda

To consider a recent interview between the Commandant of the Information Office Anti-Yellow Division, Capital Area, and General J. Adolf Koln of the Arcon First Army and Chiefs of Staff.

Present: The Chairman, C. Q. Lankowitz, current President;

Delegates: T. Chinn (Southern Provinces and Inland Seas), F. Longman (Western Sector), P. Vulmany (Eastern Sector), and R. Khan (Northern); Staff: G. Berkeley (District Captain, new appt.), and W. Loti and Mary Johnstone (Lieutenants).

The Chairman opened the discussion by explaining why a Yellow Party Council had been called and describing the recent interview he had had in his alternate capacity as Commandant of the Anti-Yellow Division, with General Adolf Koln. The Chairman played back parts of the interview from the recording made by the Yellow Party instrument, and indicated that the matter was serious in that it did represent a penetration by military intelligence into the Information Office to a depth that allowed them to establish that the Yellow Party did have some degree of control of that office. It was significant that the bribe offered by the General, i.e. that the Information Office should create the supposition that Arcon had an external enemy, which could only mean in space, was such as to appeal to the Yellow Party.

"We have slipped, gentlemen," the Chairman said, "And we can make no excuses. The party has been getting lax and inclined to take too much for granted over recent years, so that the military intelligence units set up by the predecessors of General Koln, and used with such vigor and purpose by the General himself, have scored a success of a kind not recorded for many decades. There is no question that our anti-espionage measures will have to be intensified, especially in the capital area, and a start has been made on this by our new District Captain, G. Berkeley, following the dismissal and not unexpected death of Captain Pilsen. But these matters are being taken care of, and this is not the matter directly before you.

"What is directly before you is the problem of how we shall react to General Koln's threat to make substantial allegations against the Information Office. You will be aware that should such allegations be made to the cabinet they would do little harm, since most of the politicians concerned are already well aware of what we are, but the fact must be faced that General Koln is a man of such character that he might well make his material public, in which case the suggestion that the Information Office has been penetrated by Yellows, the very party which it is designed to suppress, will cause such public indignation that members

47

of the government will have to take notice of it lest the opposition Green Party seek to make capital out of it."

Delegate F. Longman said, "We delegates from the outer regions cannot allow the Chair to pass over the surely criminal negligence of the Capital Division which has allowed a security penetration of such magnitude as to put the whole party in peril." The new captain of the Capital Division, G. Berkeley, assured the delegate that steps were being taken, and explained his own vigorous actions since he had taken office, after which this part of the discussion was ruled out of order by the Chair.

Delegate R. Khan then said that, disastrous as the events associated with Captain Pilsen had been, surely they need not look at the situation as entirely gloomy. The General had not only made a threat, he had also offered them an opportunity, by allowing them to invent an external enemy for Arcon, and so allow the army to start a secret space program, which was more fortunate in the light of Yellow Doctrine than anything that had happened in a hundred years.

Delegate T. Chinn then rose to say that it was all very well for R. Khan to speak in that way, but they must face the facts. What the General was suggesting was not a space program controlled by Yellows and in accordance with Yellow Doctrine, but some purely spurious objective, the sole purpose of which would be to allow the army to increase its estimates and construct expensive installations in secret places to counter a threat which they knew in advance to be nonexistent. That was not Yellow Doctrine but a mockery of it, and the General must know that by suggesting it he was adding insult to injury.

Delegate F. Longman asked if that was so. No one felt more strongly than he did that this situation should not have arisen, but if the army did allow them to get in the thin edge of the wedge of a space program, however spurious, could they not turn it to their own advantage? He felt that if the Chairman had pursued this matter with sufficient energy and intelligence, then they might well have ended up with a genuine space program, however limited, in which they, by use of ingenuity and the well-known political methods, could play their part.

Delegate P. Vulmany said that, much as he appreciated

Delegate F. Longman's desire to attack the Chair, he doubted if it did any good to F. Longman or anyone else.

The Chairman intervened to say that he wished to point out that General Koln's language at the meeting had been about pieces of cake, and that while matters were in that vague, initial and necessarily diplomatic stage, it would have been unwise to attempt any detailed planning. That could come later, when the Council had made up its mind.

Requesting the patience of the Council, P. Vulmany then said that if they looked at the matter clearly they would see that they had three matters before them. First was the question of whether they could in fact convince the government that there was an external threat from space to Arcon. In view of the fact that in five hundred years there had been absolutely no activity in space around Arcon, that might be difficult. Then there were the questions of whether they could turn a spurious space program into a real one, and whether they could somehow get the Yellow Party into control of it, despite the army. He asked the Staff to comment.

Captain G. Berkeley then rose to ask the Council to let him try to do exactly those things. Since this matter had arisen, he had had a small team working on it, comprising Lieutenants W. Loti and Mary Johnstone, and they had ideas. The enormous advantage of the General's offer was that to begin with it would look like they were conveying information to the government from which the army and not themselves would benefit. That would be enough to convince any politician. They had also to remember that politicians were incapable of sifting scientific data. The security surrounding the project would also be sufficient to enable the Information Office to intervene massively at every stage. In short, it was tricky, and they would have to play it by ear, but if the Council was willing to give him the authority, he was game to try it, and risk his reputation to reinstate the Capital Division.

Mary Johnstone rose to make a personal statement, saying how emotionally moved she was by an opportunity to do something real for Yellow Doctrine, and pleading with the Council to give a chance to Captain Berkeley, who was of the highest character. Regretting that time was short, the Chairman intervened to ask the Staff to withdraw.

When the Staff returned the record showed that a motion for positive action was taken and passed on the Chairman's casting vote.

XV

IT WAS NO USE looking on the black side of it, Len thought when he found himself placed with eleven other students in a guarded waiting room at the back of the Hexagon building on the fringe of Davis City. If anything unpleasant was to happen to them, it clearly wasn't yet, in the busy official area, with planes arriving and taking off every few minutes; so the thing to do obviously was get to know the people he was with, and hear their stories.

A blonde girl was talking to another with long black hair. A much tinier blonde was sitting with a big man on one of the waiting room seats, obviously waiting for something to happen. Two young men were in earnest conversation. Some of the young men were just standing around the walls looking as though they had been pushed around a little and resented it, and two girls with brown hair and one redhead also looked as though, given a chance, they would make some kind of protest. After looking at the expressions, Len frowned, thinking that these people looked more like him in their reactions than the average run of students.

He was not altogether sure that twelve people like himself would be a good idea. It might be a few too many.

He tried one of the bigger, brown-haired frowning girls who happened to be nearest. "Any idea where they're sending us, or what we're supposed to do?"

"Search me," she said with some asperity, and Len could only reflect she had probably told him all she knew.

It may not be altogether easy to control this crowd, Len thought after looking them over. He knew he himself was not always easy to control, as Gorlston had discovered, and sure enough, when a sergeant opened the door and said, "Come on out to the plane," no one moved.

Len found himself catching the eye of a large fair-haired young man across the room, and when the sergeant decided to send some soldiers in to get them, Len and the blue-eyed man moved simultaneously and blocked the door by obeying the sergeant just as the soldiers were coming in.

Whatever the students in that room were, they were not slow to see situations or make up their minds about them.

50

Apparently the door blocked itself by accident, but it stayed blocked for quite a time, and the sergeant's language did not improve things. Some of the girls proved more awkward than the men. The redhead complained loudly about both the soldiers and the sergeant, yet when Len glanced at her a moment later, she was grinning with some secret satisfaction, as though she had been looking for a way to fight back for a long time.

All right, Len thought. The guard placed on them had looked over-elaborate at first sight, but now he was not sure it was.

But they walked out to the plane on the army airfield calmly, and Len tried to get to know the people and why they were there. "I'm Len Thomas from this town," he told a slim young man. "Are you from around here?"

The young man kept his voice down and glanced at the soldiers. "David Ropotsky. This Davis City?" He said much without apparently being able to say anything, and he seemed to have more experience of the kind of transport they were getting than Len had.

He was visibly sizing up the situation and making up his mind on it, including the big long-range transport to which they were led, and when the little blonde showed a lot of leg on entering, he glanced at Len and said, "Why the girls?"

Len nodded. He had been thinking things over too, and if one feature of the situation was to be picked out, he thought that a highly intelligent remark.

The sunset was glowing over the airfield when they got into the aircraft. The soldiers stood all around the aircraft pointing weapons at it. Len knew they had had a little trouble, but all the same they seemed to be going to absurd lengths. When they got inside the aircraft, it was worse.

Some of the guards had got into the aircraft before them and were evidently intending to accompany them. They had set up a canister-type spray-gun in the front of the plane, pointing aft, and another in the back of the plane pointing forward. The only place for the twelve to sit was in the middle seats, between the two guns. Len felt contrite about it, because they were now evidently going to have an uncomfortable and restricted journey. "Now look what we've done," he said to David.

David Ropotsky looked out of the windows of the plane and pretended he did not see the guards. He and Len were last aboard, and when they were in the door was closed behind them, and the engines started. Len looked out the windows too. It was not merely to watch the outside guards, who for some reason were still looking doubtfully at the plane as it moved away from them, but it was interesting to see the takeoff, and to speculate what they could about their destination when they discovered that they were heading northward, straight for the Arcon desert.

There was no destination to the north. The area was blank on all the Arcon maps.

A conversation broke out in the body of the plane. The young people were evidently observant, and the sunset gave them their direction as clearly as if they had a compass. The soldier in the fore-part of the plane yelled out, "No talking." Len looked at the soldier with interest. Even he could have told him that it was no use saying that. They would have had to use chloroform.

Len and David Ropotsky were sitting in seats near the front of the plane facing the gun. That was a penalty for coming aboard last. Ropotsky, with a taste for which Len did not blame him, looked around and sized up the situation and then turned and began to talk to the larger and more luscious blonde behind him, whom he was calling Susan.

"Not a biologist exactly, Susan. More an organic chemist, a biochemistry research student."

How wonderful to be that, Len thought. Why, from what he had heard, to be an organic chemist meant being one of the most important men on Arcon.

Susan seemed to know something of Arcon life too. "They gave you extra privileges for that, David?"

"Sure," Ropotsky said. "Such as having my telephone tapped, my friends vetted, and all my mail opened before I got it. It depends on your research being in accordance with what they call positive thinking. Have you ever tried to apply positive thinking to biochemistry?"

Susan glanced at the soldier. "Why did they send you here?"

"I made a public statement on our most advanced research techniques, and said the results were negative."

Len wondered if all the company he was in had been selected in some peculiar way. He had a word of his own with Susan. He too glanced at the soldier, and kept his voice down. "Can we do anything about this?"

Susan saw where he was looking. "Who knows?" she said. But after a moment she turned around and said something to the people in the row behind her. They

52

talked among themselves and then turned around to those in the row behind them. They looked at Len, but they seemed to think his suggestion entirely reasonable.

The fact they were under guard in an aircraft in flight did not seem to impress them as it might. Susan took it in her stride and turned back to resume her talk with Ropotsky. "That's interesting, David."

She and Ropotsky had been quick to get acquainted, and they sounded as though they were starting what might be a long and close relationship.

"I was working in the statistics office," Susan said. "What started me was when, doing some private research, I discovered that all the propaganda the Blue Party puts out is based on a misconception. You know what they say. The Blue Party insists that we will eventually adapt ourselves to Arcon, and to prove it they produce figures to show that people are living longer now."

Ropotsky took a look at the solider, and turned around while the soldier watched him. "We aren't living longer?" he asked Susan.

Susan too looked at the soldier. "But we are. Only I happen to be a mathematics student. It's true that a newborn child has a longer life-expectancy now than when our people first came to Arcon. Our postnatal clinics are a lot better now than they were then. In fact, we didn't have any clinics then. The extra life-expectancy is accounted for by the treatment of childhood diseases in the first year of life."

I seem to be learning more about Arcon too, in this company, Len thought.

"Are old people living longer?" he asked Susan.

"No."

Len looked out of the window at the remnants of the sunset and the lack of lights on the ground that was darkening away below. They were flying north, into the uninhabited part of Arcon.

They were fed. One of the soldiers was sent around with bowls of food, which appeared to be the army method of catering on their particular aircraft. It looked like being an all-night journey.

Len looked around the plane. In the center of their group, a bunch of young people had their heads together. After the meal, Ropotsky began to talk to Susan again. Len looked across the aisle to where the small blonde was sitting. After eating, she had curled up on the seat and was showing both legs instead of one. Len did not mind that, but she appeared to be asleep.

I should have got myself a seat further back in the plane, thought Len.

Susan tapped him on the shoulder. "In response to your inquiry," she said.

Len turned to her, but she glanced at the soldier and kept her voice down. "We have a big man, Duncan, right under the eye of the soldiers at the other end, who is a trainee pilot. He can't do anything. But there's a fair-haired engineer called Sorensen, in the middle there. Don't look now. He's working on it. He says it will take a little time."

Len's feelings went up a little. "Tell them to keep working on it," he suggested to Susan, and added, "I'm an applied mathematician, by the way."

Susan flickered her eyelids at him. "I'm a pure mathematician," she said, straight-faced, and turned back to her conversation with Ropotsky. Somehow, it gave Len a feeling.

And the message was not that things were impossible, but that it would take a little time. Len sat back and tried to go to sleep in his aircraft seat.

It was a pity they could not get organized before they came into the plane, he thought. He had not been in company like that before. To his surprise, he found himself capable of sleeping.

He was wakened by a nudge. It was Ropotsky that time. The time could be near dawn. Looking straight ahead, Ropotsky kept his voice down. "We have a message: would we cause a distraction, as there's liable to be a little noise."

We not merely have equanimity, Len thought. *We are polite.*

He looked around the front of the plane. The soldier in the door to the pilots' quarters had been relieved. The man was staring down the aircraft vacantly, and Len could see that anything that happened was liable to attract him. "We might sing," he suggested to Ropotsky.

"I am not very good at singing," Ropotsky said.

Nor was Len, but he thought they might try. There was also the little blonde across the gangway. Len moved to the edge of his seat and tapped her shoulder. When she woke and gave him an innocent smile, as though she had been just waiting for him to wake her, he leaned to her and said, "Do you think we can distract the soldier?"

The soldier could not hear him, but he could see him.

54

At once, he moved his gun to Len and said, "You, get back there."

The little blonde looked at Len and then at the soldier, and moved her dress a little. The soldier's eyes immediately went to her. They opened wide, and it looked as though he had to tear them away to get them back to Len. Thereafter, they performed a shuttle service.

Ropotsky burst into song. The blonde moved her legs a little more.

I do not know what kind of group of students we are, Len thought, *but we seem to have a variety of accomplishments of the worst kinds.* He waited until the soldier presented his gun full at Ropotsky and said, "Shut up, you," before he himself burst into song.

The dawn was breaking, revealing a view through the window of the dust-layers in the lower Arcon atmosphere, and the purple-tinged peaks of a long mountain range ahead of them in the uninhabited north of Arcon, when the next thing happened. Len had seen something on the mountain range that looked like a man-made tilted dish. With all his latent electronics interests aroused, Len was looking at the dish and wondering what it was, but he did not find out just then.

The plane went into an uncontrolled spin at that point.

I wonder if I was wise to ask someone to do something, Len thought as the plane went down. He could see the dark, dawn-shadowed desert spinning up toward him. *I think I was just talking,* he thought, *and I did not realize that some one of us could and would do it.*

This is most unexpected, he thought as the desert continued to come up, tilting and very quickly.

The man called Harold Sorensen must be most effective, he realized. But not a good navigator. Len himself knew that. Otherwise Sorensen would have known better than to bring the plane down a good thousand miles away from the nearest settlement that was shown on any Arcon map.

XVI

The Shopping Lists of Mary Jean Smith:

Arcon-fat butter	½ lb.
Butter	½ lb.
Cake-mix	
Arcon-fruit oranges	6
Earth-fruit oranges	6
John's medicine.	

XVII

Memorandum dated January 3, 503 A. L.:

Priority.
Cabinet.
Restricted Circulation to Senior Ministers Only.

From the Office of the Commandant, Anti-Yellow Division (Capital Area) to P. Thompason, Secretary to the Cabinet Security Council.

Dear Sir,
In accordance with instructions from the Commandant, and further to your recent correspondence with this office, I append a list of cases covering recent months.

CASE 98425: May 12, 502 A. L.
Our Western District Officers searched the premises of one George Colimore and discovered a quantity of Yellow pamphlets together with a quantity of radio receiving apparatus and an extensive antenna array behind the suspect's house. George Colimore explained this by saying he was a radio amateur interested in long-distance reception.

CASE 99378: June 3, 502 A. L.
Our Northern District Officers searching the premises of a farmer, V. Dubrovnik, found circumstances similar to the case of George Colimore. An extensive antenna array had been hidden among crops and scrubland, but despite obvious suspicion of a communications system, no transmitting apparatus was found.

CASE 10032: June 30, 502 A. L.
On discovery of a birdcage system of wires in a swamp glade in the Davis City area, our Capital District officers kept watch on the location, and in due course arrested a known suspect, P. Perron, who had concealed a small cabin containing a quantity of highly sophisticated radio equipment with great ingenuity.
Expert examination of the installations indicated that the equipment could not possibly be used for radio transmission and reception for point-to-point contact on Arcon.

Under interrogation, P. Perron confessed that his Yellow sympathies had led him to take an interest in radio astronomy, and he demonstrated the apparatus to our officers, showing that the antenna enabled him to keep watch on a certain area of the sky each night, on an amateur astronomer basis.

In all these cases the suspects were held, but the radio apparatus was destroyed, as an interest in radio astronomy was considered a minor and relatively harmless Yellow activity.

CASE 10257: September 9, 502 A. L.

This case was of a more serious nature in that a group of Yellows was involved, operating from Elizabethville on the southern sea and using an island hideout which they visited independently on weekends when ostensibly engaged in hunting and similar pursuits.

The radio apparatus was extensive, and we regret that it was destroyed by our Far Southern officers, who responded to our inquiries by stating categorically that transmitting apparatus was found and that they were convinced that they had eliminated a station in a Yellow communication chain, and they had confessions from the men concerned that this was so.

Tape recordings found on the island were forwarded to us at our request, and these were clearly identified by our experts as consisting of stellar static, amid which a high-pitched modulated signal appeared at intervals. A rather unsatisfactory photograph of the apparatus before destruction was stated by the experts to show a "spread array" capable of being tuned in on a particular area of outer space with great accuracy.

Following this case, all districts have been requested to take special note of all radio apparatus found in control of Yellow suspects, and not to destroy such apparatus until expert examination had been undertaken. So far there have been the following results:

CASE 12131: November 13, 502 A. L.

The apparatus in this instance is situated in a desert, artesian spring, settlement three hundred miles west of Davis City. As in the case of P. Perron, the suspect T. Willoughby claims that he just happened to become interested in radio astronomy, and he thus explains how he comes to be in possession of a rotatable summer house, the roof of which forms a steerable bowl antenna. Very careful examination of papers found in the receiver room indicates that Willoughby kept watch on a star called Vista over a period of several months.

CASE 12956: December 2, 502 A. L.

Situated over a series of fish tanks only six miles from the outskirts of Davis City, and at first sight looking like the electrical and telephone supply system of a creek farm, this apparatus, found in the possession of one E. Gordini, is now being continuously operated by our technically qualified officers.

Though non-steerable, the apparatus locates on the star Vista every nine to eleven days, and despite static, signals have been detected corresponding to the tapes obtained in Case 10257, though the precise significance of this is yet to be determined.

In view of the nature of these cases, I am asked to stress to you the lack of knowledge in this office regarding the space around Arcon, and in particular the fact that we have no knowledge at all of the star Vista.

You will be well aware that our knowledge of the region of space in which our world exists is based entirely on old records of the voyage of the spaceship from Earth, which arrived at Arcon out of the continuum and did not investigate the space around it. Since this time, space investigation has been suppressed on Arcon, so that the only work done in this direction has been done illegally by Yellows. We have to admit that in this respect the Yellow Party must be far in advance of us, and it is likely that they have information not available to us, or through us, to yourselves.

The possibility that the Yellows should have discovered life on another world in our vicinity may be remote. But that they should have had transmitting apparatus attached to one of their radio telescopes, and that they might be attempting to communicate with such alien life for their own ends, could have such frightful consequences for the rightful government that we must draw it to your attention.

Should you wish us to pursue this matter we would ourselves set up a radio telescope economically, under absolute security, in a remote part of Arcon, and make further reports. At present we have to go through the expensive and cumbersome prodecure of submitting recordings to the services laboratory, thus involving outside persons in this delicate internal security matter.

Yours respectfully,
G. Berkeley (Capt.)
Acting under the Commandant
Anti-Yellow Division Records.

XVIII

The Shopping Lists of Mary Jean Smith:

See the Doctor about John.
One-quarter pound best steak.
One-quarter pound cheap cut.
Inquire price of Pulmony's Anti-Arcon Elixir*

*Ask Debby to confirm name.
Did it make her Tom live longer?

XIX

SECRET. RESTRICTED.

The Hexagon,
June 3, 503 A. L.

Memo from Army Chiefs of Staff Committee,
To:
The Secretary, Cabinet Security Council.

Sir,

The Chiefs of Staff Committee has authorized me to forward to you the enclosed technical report by the Services Electronics Laboratory on the recordings sent to us by the Information Office, receipt being as usual delayed.

At the same time, the Chiefs of Staff have asked me to express to you their grave alarm, in view of the nature of the report, that this matter should still be in the hands of the Information Office. Nothing short of the Office's incompetence could make them suggest that a recording allegedly obtained from the star Vista should be treated as an internal security matter.

As you will see from the enclosed report, the star Vista, distant twenty light-years, must be counted as one of our stellar neighbors. Nothing is known about this star except that it was not on the path by which the starship from Earth approached Arcon; and no space research has been done since.

The nature of the signals themselves, being a frequency-modulated carrier wave, do not coincide with any known natural phenomena.

The modulations of the signal consist of non-rhythmic but by no means formless waves of complex character at or above the limits of human audibility. The signals appear in high speed groups, certain sequences being repeated almost exactly at irregular intervals. This would correspond either with such words as "the" or "and" being repeated in human speech, or with conventional symbols used in a sequence of messages in code.

It would be quite impossible for these repeated signals to appear in random waves of a natural or accidental origin.

It is impossible to disregard these signals on the general grounds of "not our business," since the reception of the waves over a distance of twenty light-years must indicate either that they are beamed in our direction, or that they originate in a source of incalculable power. On the first hypothesis, the signals could only be a series of code or "speech" messages beamed to a spacecraft in the vicinity of the Arcon solar system. On the second hypothesis, the power required to broadcast such signals in all directions indicates a resource and a technology that, even at a distance of twenty light-years, must be regarded as a major threat to Arcon.

The Chiefs of Staff therefore ask me to request that a full meeting of the State Emergency Council be called as soon as possible. Your attention is drawn to the inescapable fact that, in order to be received on Arcon, these signals must have been broadcast twenty years ago.

Your obedient servant,
Q. X. Valteufel (Col.)

Enclosures: *Technical Report,*
Commentary on same.

XX

IT WAS NOT only the blue early-morning sky over the far-horizon waste of the rolling Arcon desert that was blue, Len noticed. The gently-sloping sides of the hills were streaked with it. He had not been lost in the desert before.

When he examined the aircraft, which had put its nose in the sand, it did not look likely it would take off again, so he stood around with the groups, encouraging one another and talking.

"I suppose we could have done better," Sorensen said,

looking dubiously at the distances across the desert and the fact that it was likely to be a long distance to anywhere without the plane.

"A little," Duncan said. Duncan was the big-bodied trainee pilot Len had heard about, and he looked at the aircraft with an expression of regret.

Sorensen's lazy blue eyes lightened. He had thought of something to exculpate him. He looked at Len with a sense of humor. "Someone did suggest that we do something."

"How did you do it?" Len asked.

"With a jackknife through the cabin floor. Those control pipes are difficult when you don't know how much to let out of the hydraulic fluid."

They stood around in the morning sunlight in the desert, as though they lived there, Len thought. It was the plane crew who seemed to regard the whole thing as most unfortunate.

"I wouldn't do it that way next time," Duncan explained to Sorensen. "When you break the hydraulic lines like that, you don't know if you'll get the elevators or the tail plane. The better way to bring down an aircraft is to cause an electrical short-circuit or start a little fire."

"I'll remember that," Sorensen said.

Looking at the tracks the plane had made across the desert between a hill and a rocky outcrop, Len thought that the pilot had been lucky. They all had.

After delivering his admonition to Sorensen, Duncan looked around like a responsible person to see what he ought to do next. He saw the little blonde, Penny, alone and out of place in the desert, and looking a little forlorn. He went and put his arm around her. "You and I have got a lot in common," Len heard him say to her as they went away together.

Duncan stood six foot three, and when he put his arm around Penny's waist, his hand came distinctly higher than it should have, but with Duncan in contact with her Penny did not seem to mind. Her back view quivered interestingly with her high-heeled walk as Duncan took her to look at the crew; a dark young man, Salford, was watching them with a spray-gun.

A desert is as good a place as any to make acquaintance with the people you've got mixed up with, Len thought.

"They'll have seen us disappear from their radar screens," he said to Sorensen. "I doubt that they'll leave us here long enough to starve."

The fair-haired engineer was evidently a man who kept his equanimity. "They'll send an expedition, you think?"

"Sometime."

"We don't want them to hurry. Don't you think it's time we made a protest? They were pushing us around a little."

Len agreed that it had been time they made a protest. "The thing about a protest," he remarked, "is that it ought to be effective."

"At least this is something they'll notice," Sorensen said.

The tall, red-haired girl came up to Sorensen, who said, "Hello, Vera." Although Sorensen could only have known Vera for a few hours, they seemed to know one another quite well, and Len moved away to look at the rest of the party.

There had been only one man injured in the crash, and he was the soldier who had been in the fore-part of the plane threatening them with a gun. When the plane had landed and tilted on its nose the dark one, Salford, had launched himself down the gangway at him, and the soldier had been unlucky. He was now being tended by a girl, Eliza Teen, who had admitted to nurses' training, and a young man, Ed Creet, who had stated he was a doctor.

Seeing the soldier laid out on a level rock, and Eliza and Ed standing nearby and discussing him as medical people did, as though the next procedure might well be an amputation, Len remarked to himself again that their party did seem to have a variety among its talents.

He looked around hopefully for a girl who was unattached, and saw the slim girl sitting on a rocky outcrop and combing her hair as though that were the normal place she performed her morning toilet. It was not difficult to get into conversation. He went to her and said, "Do you know what all this is about, by any chance?"

She said her name was Lucinda, and stopped combing her long black hair, which she allowed to fall around her shoulders. She was very slim, he noticed, and wearing an interestingly torn dress which she contrived to make look as though it were intended and had been made that way. She looked at Len calmly and said, "Do you intend to do anything about it when they come to get us?"

Len found himself thinking what a poised and pleasant girl she was.

"It depends on how they do it, I think," he remarked, looking around the desert horizon and the sky.

Lucinda too looked at the northern horizon. "Possibly with atomic cannon?"

"Be reasonable," Len suggested. "We're not as bad as that."

Lucinda was thoughtful as well as poised. "They may be facing the container difficulty. You know the theory? In the days when people used to search for a universal solvent, they found themselves much taxed by the obvious difficulty of finding an insoluble container in which to keep it."

Len considered her scientific imagery. Since the dress had been quite badly torn on landing, it was not the only thing he was comfortably able to consider. He found things began to appeal to him. "I notice we have a variety of professions. Are you a chemist by any chance?"

"No," she said, and indicated people around the party. "Ropotsky is our biochemist, and Imantha is on the inorganic side. My own work is social psychology." Their party appeared to interest her. "With a specialty in small social groups."

Len was sure she was a most useful person to have, and someone that they needed.

They looked at the people and the desert together. They remarked to one another that if no one came to fetch them, they were going to have a long time to look at both.

Len remembered the sight he had seen before landing. It was something to talk about. "Were you by any chance looking toward the mountains before we landed? I only had a quick view, but I believe I saw something there, like a tilted dish. It looked like a picture I once saw of a radio telescope, from the days when there was space research."

Lucinda said, "What would that be doing in this part of Arcon, even if it weren't illegal? Are you sure it was not a hallucination?"

"Is there any psychological reason why a hallucination should take the form of a radio telescope like a tilted dish?" Len said.

Lucinda looked at him speculatively. "I think I'll wait until I'm more wholly clothed before I answer that," she said. "It would be more profitable to consider any possible connection between our party and uninhabited mountains with a radio telescope."

Len had to admit that it was a problem which for the moment, was quite beyond him. He began to find their association with the rest of the party boring. Susan and Ropotsky had wandered away, he noticed, ostensibly to climb a knoll to see if they could see anything across the desert, though having climbed it they had disappeared on the other side. He wondered if Lucinda would accept a

63

suggestion that they do something of the same kind, for he had a strong feeling that things were developing fast between them, and he wished to take them further. Lucinda withstood his gaze rather well. He was not pleased when they were interrupted by the dark young man, Salford.

Salford had handed over his spray-gun to the girl Imantha, who was dutifully and seriously carrying out Salford's instructions about looking after their former captors. Salford himself seemed to be canvassing the party. They had already seen him approach Duncan and Sorensen, who were again examining the plane hopefully but with no visible degree of faith in it.

"Why shouldn't we load up with all the provisions we have available and set off across the desert?" Salford said.

Len and Lucinda looked at the young man who appeared to have such a stock of optimism as to be unquenchable.

"Are you feeling all right, Salford?" Len said.

"What do you mean, all right?"

Len looked away over the immensity of the Arcon desert. "I thought you might have hit your head on something when you made that dive down the plane to get that soldier."

Salford's dark face contracted. It was not so much what Len said as a general frustration he appeared to feel about their situation. "Why, you—! What are you going to do, just sit here and wait to be recaptured?"

Lucinda apparently knew his first name. "I didn't bring my walking shoes, Desmond," she said soothingly. "It would probably be easier for you to deal with things when someone brings some transport."

Salford looked at them angrily, then went away to find someone else. They saw him talking urgently to Ed Creet and Eliza Teen. Len could think of no one less likely to set off across the Arcon desert with no more than they could carry than a medical team.

"We may have trouble with that character, if we stay together," he suggested to Lucinda.

Lucinda was amicably thoughtful. "Perhaps someone else has had some trouble with him," she suggested. "Perhaps that's why he's here."

Len was again going to suggest that they move a little away from the rest of the party. He had noticed that Lucinda had been careful about her torn dress when Salford was present, and she was less careful with him. He felt he had reason to believe that she did not find him wholly unacceptable. He felt he knew the signs. But Susan and Ropotsky came running back over their knoll again.

"They look as though they have either seen something or met someone," Lucinda said.

Ropotsky and Susan were calling, waving their arms, and pointing to the north. While everyone in the party turned to look at them, something appeared, tiny and distant at first, in the sky above the knoll. It proved to be a slowly approaching flight of helicopters.

"We are about to be recaptured," Lucinda said. "You don't happen to have a safety pin, do you?"

Len offered his tie, which would at least tie things together, and Lucinda accepted it gratefully. Len helped her fix it, to which Lucinda did not object as long as the helicopters were still a long way away.

Len felt more resentful about the idea of being recaptured, and possibly ordered about, than he had. When Duncan and Sorensen walked over to talk to him, he asked them, "Can't we put up a resistance of some kind? Make a fight of it?".

Sorensen and Duncan had apparently had the same idea, but Duncan was looking thoughtfully at the helicopters now that they were getting nearer. "Two-rotor jobs," he remarked professionally. "Armored troop carriers."

They watched the helicopters perform a maneuver. They had split up into two groups, apparently with the intention of approaching them from either side. Instead of approaching them directly, they were arranging themselves in a circle around them, and going down to land.

"What are they doing?" Sorensen inquired.

"Landing," Duncan said. "To turn the armored troops on us."

"Don't they seem to be attaching a lot of importance on our party?" Len said.

"I told you," Lucinda remarked. "Atomic cannon."

"They can't think that will be necessary," Duncan said.

It was not, and they watched developments. Imantha and Salford came over with the light arms they had captured from the soldiers from the plane, but even Salford seemed torn between the realities of the situation and his desire to make a fight of it.

After the landing maneuver, one helicopter flew nearer, but stayed at a wary distance while it addressed them through a loudspeaker. The voice boomed across the desert.

"Indicate your surrender and lay down your arms, or we will commence a gas attack."

65

Salford looked at the wind conditions, which were ideal for the use of an incapacitating nerve gas. Len told Lucinda, "Your military assessment of the situation was an overestimate." Duncan looked regretful and said, "We had better surrender gracefully."

Ed Creet did not wait for their advice. Perhaps the condition of his patient had something to do with it, but he took off his white shirt and began to wave it.

The helicopter circled around them and ordered, "Split up into twos and separate. You will be picked up by transports."

Ropotsky had looked thoroughly disgusted throughout the entire proceedings. He was holding Susan's hand. "Like de-fusing an atomic bomb," he said. "They believe they only get the critical mass when they put the parts together." Then he set off back into the desert again with Susan as the armored cars approached them.

Len wondered if there was not, after all, some significance in Ropotsky's obscure remark as he and Lucinda left the rest and were approached and picked up by one of the vehicles that were coming in from all directions.

It was true it seemed quieter when he and Lucinda were isolated and traveling between armed soldiers in the back of the open vehicle, but he noticed that instead of returning to the helicopters, the vehicles had formed into a line, and were heading north across the desert. It was possible that the authorities were not trusting them in aircraft again, but he deduced from the fact that they were heading for their destination on the ground that it must be at no very great distance.

XXI

The Shopping Lists of Mary Jean Smith:
(On the torn-off corner of an unmailed letter.)

. . . Oh, Linda, dear, do forgive me for pouring out my heart to you. What will I do if John dies? How helpless I feel in this cruel world.

Love,
Mary.

Pulmony's Arcon-Check Elixir.
Two steaks, one good, one cheap.
Earth-type pure-grown fruit? PRICES!
    Sell the brooch.
    Inquire cost clean-air unit.
    See nursing-help people.

XXII

From:
George Barault,
Consulting Engineer,
Davis City,
June 15, 503 A. L.

To:
Commandant C. Q. Lankowitz,
Information Office Headquarters,
By Messenger.

Dear Commandant,

Most certainly I value our connection, and I hope that the Information Office will continue to use my consultant service from time to time. I cannot say how highly I attach importance to our mutual trust, especially on a personal basis, of absolute discretion.

It was just that I hesitated to commit myself to writing on such a matter. As it is, now that I have made the investigation you asked of me, and assuming that you and the army are committed to this project, I doubt if you will really want to show these results to anyone, as you said you might.

The truth is that Arcon's capacity for flights to other stars is as it always has been. You know as well as I do that the knowledge was brought from Earth, and, in your own files and archives, you must have the plans of how to construct starships of all shapes and sizes. As to industrial capacity, a hundred years ago, if the entire planet had bent its whole effort to the will, we could have done it.

But have you counted the cost? Liquid oxygen for the lift-off stages alone would be a drain on our industrial supply, but the vital production of high-tensile alloys would stop the entire aircraft industry for at least a year. This kind of thing *just could not be done in secret*. You would have to involve the planet in a nation-wide effort, and confide in all the people.

What do you propose to do? You can't seriously send off one man, and anything else would be a sham, and I am at a loss because I don't know your political motives.

Forgive my apprehension,
George Barault.

XXIII

The Shopping Lists of Mary Jean Smith:

One steak

I can see

him every time I close my eyes.
One bread
One

One . . .

If I went to the park, I could sit and look at the children's fountain.

One

The children too will die that way. Looking at them, and watching them play in the city park, I would count their seconds by my pulse-beat.

I am thirty-five. No shopping this day.

XXIV

From I. O. records:
The Conference of the 22nd November. . . .

Commandant C. Q. Lankowitz left the capital on official leave and traveled, as was natural for a person in his position, to the exclusive resorts of southeast Arcon. He did not stay in one of the better-known towns on the pink-tinged beaches on the fabled southeastern sea, but in the area where the shore was broken by the bold pink and golden headlands, and it was there, where the café terraces hung high above the water, and the climbing and hanging plants partly obscured the view of the eternal sea and sky and the coves below, that he held his special conference with delegates T. Chinn of the Southern, and P. Vulmany of the Eastern regions.

For reasons of security, the conferences were held for the most part at a table on a terrace in the open air, so that the only record of the conversations consists of a recording made by T. Chinn by concealing a microphone in one of the flowering plants that decorated the balustrade by the table above the sheer drop below.

During the first day, T. Chinn and P. Vulmany inquired about the latest news from the capital, particularly regarding security and the penetration of the army into the Information Office, and hence possibly into the Yellow Party itself. Commandant Lankowitz assured them that this leak had now been firmly closed, thanks largely to the work and enthusiasm of G. Berkeley of the Capital Division, who had proved to be an extremely useful man, though about whom there were certain reservations which he would mention later.

T. Chinn inquired about relations with the army, and was told that they appeared to be satisfied with the increased estimates. P. Vulmany asked why, therefore, C. Q. Lankowitz had called them to what was virtually an emergency meeting of the inner Council.

C. Q. Lankowitz said it was because the space project to which they were committed had proved in technical and political terms impractical. As he believed they already knew or suspected, the construction of an actual stellar vehicle, capable of making a journey to a star, would require such a diversion of industrial and technical resources from Arcon industry that the whole matter would have to come to public notice.

T. Chinn remarked that this was a very serious statement, and that, as the waiter was hanging about within fifteen feet of their table, they had better order fresh drinks and get rid of him. After this was done, P. Vulmany said that to abandon the project would not only reopen the whole question of their relations with the army, but it would also have a catastrophic effect on party morale. C. Q. Lankowitz said he agreed, and that was why he had called them together as a small, experienced and inner group to discuss the matter.

Vulmany queried whether, dangerous as they knew the course was, they might not go the whole hog and make the project public, representing it as a patriotic response to an incalculable threat to Arcon. T. Chinn said that that would be difficult in view of the long-term Green and Blue propaganda against space adventures. They had long ago decided to work through the popular political parties, rather than against them. C. Q. Lankowitz said that they should remember that the whole basis of the project was the Information Office story of signals received from Vista, and that if the matter was made public every news organ and technical institute would be trying to hear the signals. In these circumstances, it would be impossible to maintain the fiction.

It was decided on the first day that security should be maintained and that since the power of the party was based on the Information Office monopoly of information,

69

no steps should be taken which would compromise that position, or which would bring matters they had control of into the area of random chance of public politics.

XXV

THEY RODE in the back of the armored car, with soldiers with guns in their hands sitting stolidly beside them as they crossed fold after fold of the rolling desert. When something began to emerge out of the haze ahead, they said nothing at first. They could see the others in the line of cars also looking ahead, making out a hillside where there seemed to be some kind of habitation, at least a line of army hutments. As they went down into a deeper dip and lost the view, Len turned to Lucinda and watched the frown and the movement of her tongue across her lips. Since their recapture, the close guard under which they were kept in the vehicles had not encouraged conversation.

Since they had been able to make out the buildings of what looked like a township on the hillside, and above it the hazy but indisputable shape of the tilted dish of a radio telescope, Len turned to a soldier.

"What is this place where you're taking us?"

The soldier looked at him, then looked ahead again. His expression was almost, but not quite, indifferent. Maybe he had been told not to talk to them, or maybe, from the way he looked, they knew too little yet. He was not keen to talk against the noise and jolting of the car. Not the amount of talk that they would need, to tell them.

They would see soon enough, the soldier's silence said, and as they traveled through a defile, rising and watching the air became clearer, Len found Lucinda's dark eyes upon him and suddenly meeting his in one long glance.

They came out of the defile, with a track leading them forward to the hills along the level ground of an escarpment, and it was all before them. They had known that there was something there, and that someone, somehow, where the mountains met the desert, must have found a source of water that would allow them to build what was virtually a township. But they had not begun to understand that there was so much of it. It was too much for one view.

There was an incredibly tall, thin, spire-like object away to their right, with its base still out of view in a place where there were also construction buildings, in a valley bottom.

70

Feeling Lucinda's touch on his hand, with a sense of the intimacy of the physical contact, Len looked ahead where she looked. She was looking at where their track went, between the valley and the hillside.

"It looks as though they have found a container that will contain us," she said, just loudly enough for him to hear and understand her.

The building toward which they were indubitably heading if they kept to the track, since it stood alone, had high walls and looked at first like a desert fortress, until Len looked more closely and saw there were considerable grounds inside the walls, surrounding a central glass-and-concrete building, the nature of which it was hard to see at first.

Since there was no one that the walls could be meant to keep out, it seemed they might be meant to keep someone in. Or maybe it was just part of the security. And security and secrecy were what the whole location of the place was meant for, if Len could believe what he was seeing.

"Look at the tall object in the valley."

The helicopters which had come to them in the desert were overhead. The flight went past them at an angle, heading for the valley, where evidently there was an airfield. Out of the valley, booming up out of the murk and heading away through the foothills in the direction of Davis City, went a heavy army transport plane. It was like a freight line from a desert factory.

"Is it . . . ? A space rocket, here on Arcon?"

She might well ask that, Len thought, looking at it while he had the chance, while they were still crossing the escarpment toward the isolated fortress-building with the grounds.

There were no space rockets on Arcon. In a way, that was the point of Arcon politics. The public of Arcon had had enough of space, after one great space adventure. The planet might have its problems, as had any world, but under the Blues and Greens, for five centuries, it was Arcon that the people had kept their minds on.

But there was something unmistakable about the tall cylinder, wide at the base and narrowing upward in successive stages, lonely, somehow forceful and erect and emphatic in those surroundings, still under construction, as they could see by movement on the skeleton gantry that stood beside it. It was a matter of trying to guess the scale of it against the foothills.

"A rocket," Len said. He looked at the soldiers, who held their weapons and looked ahead at the fortress-building.

"A deep-space interstellar rocket. And being built here in an army desert outpost."

"What are we doing here?" Lucinda said, and Len looked quickly at her.

She was still a dark slim girl in a torn dress, but her eyes were taking in the whole scene, from the radio telescope on the hill, through the white houses on the hillside, the building toward which they were heading, and the valley and the rocket. She had gripped his hand after she had touched it. Her mind was moving quickly, seeking the essential points of the situation with which she was confronted. She glanced quickly at the soldiers, guessing how far they could talk in front of them.

Len thought: *In the lottery of our twelve, I seem to have drawn more than a pretty figure.*

Her eyes had narrowed on what they could see of the valley. "You think it is an interstellar rocket?"

"I'm no expert, Lucinda," Len said dryly. *Who was, on Arcon?* "It just looks as though there are two chemical blast-off stages. The third stage is tall and long. That would be the atomics for the deep-space ion-beam propulsion. Above that, though we're too far away to see, should be landing rockets, and the living quarters in the space capsule itself, just below the nose cone."

Lucinda gave him a look which said he had told her more than she knew, or had expected. They were sitting close together in the vehicle.

"But this isn't a starship, big as a city, such as our people came here from Earth in?"

They watched the soldiers, trying to get some confirmation from them. They could not communicate with those in the other vehicles. Len looked again at the rocket as they approached the building that lay ahead, where a gate was open.

"If you look at the nose cone, you can see it can only be a small crew."

"How many?"

Len was silent, riding in the car.

He found Lucinda's eyes watching, saying she had not dropped her question. "How do I know?" he said. "Ten. Maybe twenty."

He would not fool Lucinda by avoiding twelve. It was just a wild idea. They had no need to think it, he told himself insistently. Or was it true that the men in the car with them were grinning, as much as to say, "You don't *know*"?

"We might wonder why we have been brought here,"

Lucinda said. She looked again at the almost-completed rocket. "At this stage of the proceedings."

They had to look back to look at the rocket now. They were approaching the open gate in the walls of the construction that lay ahead.

They almost lost sight of the glass-and-concrete building that lay within the walls. The whole thing was set on a desert shelf, away from the township and the valley. Over the wall, they could still see a tall thin metal tower. Through the gate, they began to see what looked like a training area within the grounds. Just before they reached the gate, Ropotsky stood up in the leading car and pointed back at the rocket, only to disappear again, evidently pulled down by the soldiers who were riding with him. Then their whole column of vehicles drove through the gate, moving more slowly through the entrace where there were sentries standing. It was impossible not to feel that they were not intended to come out of that gate again for a little time.

To Lucinda, Len said, "So this is the place we've come to."

It did not look unpleasant inside the walls. The glass-and-concrete building might have been a college wing, and beside it, welcoming in the desert, was a glint of water from a pool. The grounds had a drive through them, which their convoy was following toward the building. On each side were skeleton pieces of apparatus that looked like machines. One of them was cylindrical in shape and looked like a section of a mock-up of a rocket. The tower they had seen had wires descending from it, with a platform at the top as though it were intended for jumping in a harness for a duration of three seconds free-fall. Len stared at one piece of apparatus. It was a seat on a long arm, which was intended to rotate about a center.

The leading cars drove up and stopped at the building to discharge their passengers, and then drove off and out of the gate again. Soon they were all standing in a group, looking at the building itself, which had windows that showed them academic classrooms, and from which a man in a colonel's uniform was emerging to meet them, with a staff behind him. Duncan and Penny stood near Len and Lucinda. Duncan said, "This is a place for space-flight training."

They stood looking at men in white coats who were walking among the machines, and at the gate which the sentries were closing after the last of the vehicles had gone out again. No one had told them which way to go. If the place

73

was intended for space-flight training, they could see no students in it, except themselves.

"So you are our volunteers," the colonel said. He had stopped to survey them ten yards from them. "I am told you had already wrecked the plane before you got here. It's not a good beginning."

It was a little later, when they were in the building, after they had eaten and washed and he had had them assembled in a classroom, that he gave them what he called his introductory lecture.

"Don't ask me why you in particular are here. I didn't choose you. That was in the hands of the Information Office, and it is not for me to say if they made a good job of it. It is sufficient that you are here, and we have to work together."

From the low dais on which he stood, with a man in a white coat beside him, he looked them over.

"The situation is this. Some time ago, the Information Office told us that they had discovered that the Yellows had begun to take an interest in radio astronomy, and in particular in a star called Vista. It is neither your business nor mine to know the how and why. It is sufficient that radio signals were coming from the vicinity of Vista, which is twenty light-years from Arcon, and the Yellows, our own anti-government party, have tried to communicate with the signals' senders.

"As you know, we on Arcon are very ignorant of the stellar space around us. Since the Landing, all our energies have been used on Arcon and we have had neither the means nor the incentive to look beyond our own solar system. It was natural that we should assume that, as far as intelligent life went, the space around us was wholly empty."

The colonel, whose name they had learned was Glasson, surveyed them thoughtfully, in a singularly grim way.

"The situation is different now. For the security of our world, it is essential that we should know something of this Vista planet. We cannot send radio probes, for the signals needed to control them would alert Vista of our intentions, and of our presence if the Yellows have not already done that damage for us. There must therefore be a manned flight, and that is where you come in. What you have been selected for is to be the space crew."

He watched their reactions to his statement as though wondering if they already knew it. He did not dislike the telling.

But he did not sound as though that was the end, or the worst, of what he had to tell them.

"There are difficulties about that too. Arcon is not a wealthy planet. I presume I had better tell you this. We cannot provide you with a rocket that will reach a very high proportion of the speed of light. You will not get very much shrinkage of the universe or time-dilation such as occurs at C-speeds. Your journey of forty light-years, to and from Vista, where you will orbit the planet when you find it, and photograph its surface, will take forty years of your time. That is why you are evenly divided as to sexes, so that should you not survive the voyage, your children will bring the spaceship back, and the photographs you will have taken of this world."

It was a moment before it hit them.

Whatever else they had expected on coming into the space school in the desert, it was not what the colonel had just said, that they would spend their lives in the rocket, traveling just near enough to the speed of light for the time difference to compensate for the amount by which they did not achieve that speed.

Len tried to envisage them, old as they would be by then, and near the death-age by Arcon time, arriving at a strange solar system, seeing the planets come up, hearing radio signals, and trying to photograph an alien world. Then, after that, and even supposing they were successful, turning back to Arcon to fly homeward to a world they would never live to reach.

Their questions burst out on the colonel. There was Eliza Teen's voice rising above the rest. "Do you mean the girls are expected to have children in this rocket?"

For some reason, the colonel on the platform in the classroom looked as though he enjoyed telling them. "I think it will happen," he said. He looked at the six girls and the six men. "It would be surprising if it didn't."

He held up a hand when the girls called out to him, and Salford in particular began to have his say. To find out what was before them, they had to listen to the colonel.

"Understand this," he said. "You were selected by the Information Office for this work, no doubt for their own good reasons. And you can't do anything about it. Your rocket will be kept under radio control for as long as they consider it safe to do so. At the space school here you will be working not only for the project but for your own survival. You know the facts now and, from the Information Office, I understand you volunteered for it."

With that, he stepped down from the platform and left the classroom, and they were taken to their separate rooms inside the space school, with armed guards to see they went there.

XXVI

From I. O. records:

C. Q. Lankowitz was the first at the table with the view of the cove through the hanging vines when the conference was resumed the following morning. He indicated the mid-morning view of the sunlight over the placid southeastern sea, and complimented the others on the way in which they merged with the background of wealthy vacation people at the hotel, and asked them if they had changed their positions overnight.

T. Chinn ordered fruit juice when the waiter came, and said he would not have as much to drink that day as he had had the previous night. P. Vulmany said, "If I remember correctly, we got ourselves into a deadlock. We could not make the space project public, lest the information on which it is based be questioned, or in case we might lose control of it. Yet we have to keep it to save the party."

C. Q. Lankowitz said that the morale and the strength and enthusiasm of the party must be their overriding consideration. That was what they were there for. It was because the party needed it that he had accepted General Koln's gambit, when the General had come, as he thought, to force him into it. That had been despite the fact that he knew he was embarking on a dangerous course. He instanced once again G. Berkeley, typical of the good men in the party, whom he had had reason to believe might have become dissatisfied with the present leadership, and might even have led a move to challenge it, but whose whole attitude had been changed since then.

P. Vulmany said that he agreed that anything presenting a challenge to the present leadership was indeed the most serious matter of all that they had to deal with.

T. Chinn remarked that in that case they had to sustain a space-shot when it was impossible to sustain a space-shot, and it seemed to him that it would take considerable experience to do this.

C. Q. Lankowitz said that it was not a space-shot, but a space project that they had to sustain, both to satisfy the party, avoid any possible threat to the leadership, and maintain their relationship with the army. He had naturally given the matter a little thought before he came to them.

The advantage of security had always seemed to him important. When dealing with classified material this was particularly so. Various design teams were working on the rocket. He had thought it better that they should be kept out of touch with one another. It was also better if the purchasing of prefabricated items and systems from industrial firms was handled by the Information Office. It would be better if the construction teams were insulated from one another, and also from the design teams.

P. Vulmany asked what that meant.

C. Q. Lankowitz said that a certain scaling down of items of the project might take place at certain stages, and this would be facilitated if the overall plans for the rocket were handled exclusively by his office. For instance, the requirements for an atomic drive motor for a deep-space project were exceptionally severe. If these were scaled down, the item would be far less bulky, which in turn could mean a considerable reduction in the lift-off stages. A project would then become feasible both without too much disruption of Arcon industry and within the limitations of secrecy.

T. Chinn said he was not too sure what that meant, but he felt he would have to reserve his position on it, and think a little.

P. Vulmany said it would be unfortunate if things were like that. He had always cherished certain ideals throughout his life. He did not think he was a very sentimental person.

C. Q. Lankowitz said no one felt that more than he did, but they had to be realistic. The army could be told, for example, that the rocket would take two generations to get there and back. And it was more convenient that way. For if it took a longer period for the journey than the number of light-years involved, then, if as a consequence of the alterations the rocket did not come back at all, there was a chance it would be forgotten. Or it could be said to have fallen to the enemy, which would give them the excuse for another space project someday, which would be good for the Yellow Party, which was their main objective.

XXVII

From the army report on the uprising:

The records show that General Koln did not take official leave in the autumn of 503 A. L. Instead, he used his leave period to visit various army units at a distance from the capital, making wide-ranging flights to distant units, including a journey to see the desert survey group then operating in the far north of Arcon in the desert. This was the group which had chosen the site and which was working on the primary installations of the rocket project.

It is now known that this is the time that the General began to gather a few of the higher ranking army men around him. The process was necessarily delicate, since at that time the General could show his hand to no one, but how it was done has been described in the testimony of the then commander of the desert survey group, who was later retained in charge of the project site throughout, a Colonel Glasson.

They were standing by the project camp watching a party of Information Office technicians setting out across the near-by hillside. It was because they were Information Office men that the colonel looked at them indignantly and took the opportunity to speak to the General.

"Sir, I thought this was to be our show."

"Our show?" the General said.

"Our survey," the colonel said. "Our space school, our rocket project, our rocket, our space-shot."

The General stood looking at the Information Office technicians who were laying out the site for the radio telescope by driving red and white poles into the uneven ground of the hill above them. It was true that the army did seem to have been reduced to a supporting role of bringing in supplies, arranging transport and doing the earth-moving, while all the more technical and interesting work was being done by the men with Information Office flashes.

It was true that in the scene around them the rock-shifting, road-making, ground-leveling and foundation-digging was very heavy work in the desert heat, and the army seemed to be doing it. "Colonel," the General said. "Are you sure you haven't got a chip on your shoulder?"

"Me?" said Colonel Glasson. "I am completely unprejudiced." He looked in a slightly strangled way at a group of his best soldiers who were digging a trial trench under the eye of an Information Office technician who had had a small awning erected so that he could sit in the shade to watch them. "It's just that as far as the Information Office is concerned, I hate everything to do with them, including their guts," he said.

The General looked more thoughtful. "Come with me, Colonel," he said.

He took the colonel with him across the camp and to the helicopter-landing where the General's pilot climbed promptly out of the General's helicopter and stood to attention.

"All ready and correct to take off for your inspection of the higher valley, sir!" the pilot said, saluting.

"Thank you, sergeant," the General said. "But I won't need you today. I have decided to pilot the machine myself, and the colonel will come with me."

"Sir," said the pilot. "The helicopter will carry three."

The General looked at the dreadful, dust-filled landscape. "That's all right, sergeant," he said. "You take a day off today. Amuse yourself."

He and the colonel got into the helicopter and flew away from the hell of the digging operations toward the peace of the higher valley.

They did not in fact do much inspection of the higher valley, about which the colonel could tell the General in expressive and malevolent detail as they flew. As soon as they were out of sight of the camp, the General set the machine to climbing, and when they came to rest it was on the summit of one of the peaks around the valley sides, where the air was cooler.

There was also no one to overhear them within a score of miles on that peak, and they could sit peacefully in the helicopter with the window open and look out with a bird's eye view over the rolling wastes of Arcon.

"Now you can talk to me, Colonel," the General said.

"I don't see why our rocket project, which was invented and designed for us, should be infiltrated by the bloody Information Office and taken over at all its important points," the colonel said.

"It is said to be reasonable," the General said. "Since the project is to be kept secret, and since the construction of the propulsion systems and the prefabrication of the rocket sections has to be handled by civilian firms before everything is flown out here, the Information Office naturally sees it as an internal security matter."

"To hell with that," the colonel said. "From what you told me last night, about which I've been thinking, it seems to me that you started this thing to be able to give a solid reason to the government for army expansion, but, with all due respect, sir, the Information Office has out-maneuvered you at all important points when it comes down to detail."

"What detail?"

"The I. O. is to design the rocket, place the contracts,

do technical assembly, select the space crew, train them and run the radio telescopes. The army is reduced to the role of hewers of wood and drawers of water."

The General considered the colonel's mastery of detail and essential competence despite an outlook on life that was as pessimistic as it was prejudiced.

"What would you think, Colonel, if I told you I have let the Information Office seem to out-maneuver me in order that they should think me a brash general who is also a little stupid?"

The colonel stiffened.

"Sir, I would ask you what we hope to get out of it."

"Control?" the General suggested. "Suppose, just suppose, I was to indicate that what we might get out of it ultimately was complete army control of Arcon?"

The colonel gazed away at the endless, blue-tinged hillsides of his planet's wastes, but he looked at them as though they were a green landscape of grass and streams and valleys all filled with roses.

"I'd say I was your man, sir."

"It could be dangerous, Colonel. This is working up to an event that ought to be spectacular."

"That's what I came into the army for, sir, in my mistaken youth. For glory not unmixed with a hint of danger."

"Don't change your spots suddenly, Colonel. Don't suddenly become a friend of the Information Office. Just continue in your old way."

"Sir," said the colonel. He sat by the General as though scenting a flowered air and hearing a faraway sound of bells across the rocky hill slopes. "Can you give me any hint, even a hint, of what the outcome of this is going to be?"

The General glanced at him and wondered how much he had to tell such an emphatic man, to gain his undying support and loyalty and keep him happy.

"It's true I started this project, Colonel, but the position we want to get ourselves in is one where we can eventually disown it."

"Disown it, sir?"

"Space ventures are unpopular on Arcon," the General said cryptically. "You want to think about that, Colonel." He put his hand to the helicopter starter button. "Especially if the public should eventually get to know of it."

The noise of the helicopter motor cut into whatever the colonel had been about to say, which was something about "the common people," and he looked instead with wonder at the Arcon landscape as they flew back to the project camp.

He was wondering, he reported later, just how the General proposed, despite the Information Office control of security, to convey the news of the project to a sufficient number of the Arcon people, and how he could so do it as to insure the overthrow of Arcon democracy. That would surely depend on how it was presented, he thought, and that, without question, would have to be in a dramatic form.

XXVIII

AFTER THE colonel's introductory lecture, Len was conducted to his room to contemplate the job for which he was in the space school, and for which Berkeley had sent him.

It was a clean room, with a bed, bright walls, a chair, a window, and a student's desk.

Len stood by the window. He could see two men, instructors in white coats, walking in the grounds. Outside the grounds, over the wall, he could see the barren peaks of Arcon's northland. He hardly saw the scene. Len was human. He saw the firm delicacy of Lucinda's features in his mind's eye, and the curve of her breasts as revealed by the dress that had been torn on landing. The pictures merged.

He found he was standing with clenched fists. Too much was happening to him at one time. He looked down at the desk. There were books on the desk, and one of them was called *The Principles of Three-dimensional Navigation,* and the other was *Electronics Applied to Space Flight*.

Len went and flung himself down on the bed. He looked fixedly at a blank wall. He thought of himself and Lucinda in the rocket, then rejected the thoughts that came to him. He did not know why he did so. The whole situation in the space school, it seemed to him, lacked some inner logic. He thought of the tall spire of the rocket that stood in the valley beyond the space school walls. His mind fought and searched for something. He looked at the other walls of his room, as though looking for something that was not there.

It was not so much fury he felt, while he was in his room, as a hopeless longing. It was true that his thoughts were full of unanswered questions. There was too much doubt. Berkeley, and the way he had come to the space school. What could he do about it? What had he ever succeeded in doing, and was he not just a helpless pawn in a game someone else had chosen?

His mind filled again with the picture of Lucinda as he had first seen her in the desert, with the torn dress revealing too much as she put up her arm to comb the dark hair that fell about her shoulders. Suddenly, inexplicably, he smiled a little.

The door of his room opened. A soldier stood in the doorway looking at him. "You can come out to eat now."

Len got up and faced the soldier. *And they call us space volunteers,* he thought. The man turned away and went to another door along the corridor. In the corridor, Duncan and Sorensen and Ropotsky were already out. Beyond the stair head, where there was a sentry, they could see the girls leaving their rooms. Sorensen looked at Len with a lazy glance. Duncan's gaze drifted over him. Ropotsky moved around them. Len's feelings contracted.

"We are going into space under radio control," Ropotsky said to Len. "They will direct us on course by radio until we are well on our way to Vista?" He watched Len. Len looked back and shook his head. Sometimes Ropotsky talked too much.

"Let's go," Duncan said.

Ed Creet and Salford were being let out of their rooms. The girls came toward them. Looking at the party, Len had the same feeling he had had in the desert and in the aircraft. They moved on down the corridor.

Even looking at the back of the men's heads, Len still felt it. It was these men and these six girls who were coming past the sentry.

Lucinda halted, waiting for him at the stair head. The sentry looked as though she should go on. She wore a new dress, green and plain. It had been in her room, where they all had clothes. Someone had anticipated their requirements and knew their sizes. That had been prepared too, in advance, along with all the other items of the project. She turned around to show it to Len while Susan was going to Ropotsky and Imantha was walking with Salford down the stairway. She said, "Maybe you prefer the torn one?"

"Yes," said Len. In a way it was pointless to talk. A kind of invisible barrier had sprung into being around the whole party. Too much was understood.

At the bend of the stair, a window looked out in the direction where, over the wall, they could see the thin spire of the rocket in the valley. Little Penny and Eliza Teen, with Duncan and Ed Creet in attendance, were looking at it. Eliza said, "What are we supposed to do in that?" and Penny said, "I know what we are supposed to do."

The girls laughed. The guards and sentry who were watching them looked uneasy. There was something sharp about the girls' laughter.

Len felt a fierce exultation burn through him. It was there. Something had happened, and someone, somewhere, had not got a clue. Yet it was still, at that stage, something completely vague and undefinable, like people meeting.

"Don't look like that, Len," Lucinda said, and they went down, to the dining room.

They could talk there, at the table. It was not intended. The soldiers were to wait on them at table, which was no doubt intended to prevent them from wandering off and losing themselves in kitchens. Someone had decided it was best to keep an eye on them, even there. But when the soldier brought the soup course no one ate, and Salford sat staring at him as long as he stood by them. The soldier backed away, and then they ate. Slowly, it was as though they built an invisible ring around them.

Ed Creet talked into his soup. It was a low voice that would not carry to a soldier, and everyone was watching. "Supposing we aim to do it, how would we get out of here?"

Even Ed Creet knew it, and was talking about possibilities. It was something of a surprise to Len. He had thought of a lot of things, but not actually of getting out. He examined the idea. It was fairly worthless.

Eliza bent her head to the contents of her plate. "They have a sentry in the corridor. There are the building guards, and the walls, and a thousand miles of desert." She sounded reluctant, as though saying play it on the home ground.

Salford looked down the line of girls. "The sentry looks sex-starved," he said softly. "All the guards are lost in the desert."

Len wondered what he wanted.

"The sentry has a spray-gun," Ropotsky said.

"Anyone who had a spray-gun here could get two," Salford said. He looked at a soldier's belt. The soldier was coming to take the plates.

They did not talk when a soldier was near them. They watched the soldiers waiting on table, steadily.

Ropotsky must have been thinking what Salford meant. When the soldier had gone, he said, "So you take the building."

Duncan shifted his shoulders indifferently. "We don't want the building. We would want the gates."

They mean it, Len thought.

83

Sorensen tried to stop it. "The air strip is three miles away."

"Len's room," Salford said.

"Len's?"

"He has a view of the gate. He can see what time the guard is changed."

"So?"

"It is midnight. We are waiting there, armed. Then we have a vehicle."

Salford was a difficult man to stop. They had seen it.

"Face it, Des. If we got away in a plane, we would be shot down before we got to Davis City."

"You think so? There are twelve of us. We have the armament first of the interior guard, then of the new guard coming to relieve them. It is night, and we move fast in the vehicle. We cut communications first. We drive into the airfield firing."

An image of the rim of the Arcon desert came into Len's mind, and the thousands of miles of desert to lose a plane in. While the soldiers passed along the table, they thought about it. It could work. They would end with the plane lost in some swamp-creek jungle somewhere.

"Twelve people working hard could bury a plane," Ropotsky said.

Lucinda had been watching them. Like Len, she had been seeing if they were serious or not. The answer was that it did not matter if they were serious. For some reason, when Len looked at Lucinda's face, he seemed to see things through her eyes. It was like watching some newborn, clumsy, twenty-four-legged animal taking its first steps. That was the way Lucinda was looking at the group, as though she had learned some kind of a lesson in the desert aircraft crash.

"And then?" she said. "We live like naked outlaws, on some swamp-sea, in the jungle somewhere?" She spoke as quietly as the rest, just keeping her head down, making her contribution.

Len's eyes narrowed. He was the only one who had been watching her before she spoke. She was not a girl asking. She was not even a woman pouring cold water on a young man's scheme.

More like an experienced operator, it looked to him, doing something she had to do.

One of the civilian instructors suddenly came to sit with them. They could not talk any more. The instructor looked uneasy. He said, "You may not understand this. We instructors want to cooperate with you when you work for your survival."

After a while, on behalf of all of them, Duncan said, "Yes?"

"You have to work," the instructor said.

Duncan was silent. Len looked around, waited, and replied of his own accord: "We want more information."

There was the uneasy look again. "You do. We know you do. This evening you'll get an Information Office briefing."

Neither Len nor any of the others replied to that. They had all had experiences of one kind or another with the Information Office. After a while, the instructor seemed to recognize their coolness. He went away.

"Is an Information Office briefing different from an army briefing?" Ropotsky said. Len noticed the way Duncan's eyes went to him, as though it was something for speculation.

From the dining room, they went to the lounge, which had comfortable chairs and a wide window looking out on the swimming pool. It looked as though it would be a better place to talk than the dining room, for it was not as formal and they could be at ease in it; in fact, because of the placing of the chairs, they were more distributed around the room, and a soldier-servant was constantly present. He would bring drinks or coffee, but when they sent him for them another appeared while he was gone, going around to empty the ash trays, which did not need emptying.

They had been there about an hour when a youngish woman came in. She had a sheaf of papers with her, and she looked at them and then went over to the window while they watched her. She examined the area outside the window, then stood looking at their soldier-servant. He looked at her, and then went out and closed the door behind him. Len and Lucinda were sitting together, and she touched his hand.

The Information Officer, Len realized, and looked at the woman again. He had not seen a female Information Officer before. She had a competent, well-formed face, but an emotional look about the eyes that he had noticed in certain women. She went to a chair at a table, in a position near the center of the room. Her voice was firm.

"Would one of you check the door and see that the soldier has gone away as he should have? I would like two more of you to sit by the window and watch the outside. Apart from that, you can gather around me."

They had not intended to do anything for an Information Office representative, except that she turned out to be a woman. Ropotsky went to the door, looked out, and closed it. Ed Creet and Sorensen moved to places by the window. Nothing was quite what they expected, inside the space school.

"My name is Mary Johnstone," she told them. "I am from the Information Office, but this will be news to you: I also am a Yellow. There is a very considerable amount you do not know yet. Let me tell you the most important things first. This space project is not what you think it is, nor what the army has told you. We control it, because we control the radio telescope, and our aims are Yellow aims.

"As far as we are concerned, the army story about this project is just a convenient cover. We have no intention that you should spend your lives in a rocket flying to and from Vista. That is unnecessary, because you have been selected as a pioneer party who will go to found a new colony on a Vista planet, and not come back. This will allow us to send you out at maximum power on the outward journey. The journey will be a long one, but because you will be able to fly much closer to the speed of light, it will last only a year or two of your time."

It was something that was more of a shock to them than the colonel's story had been. It was the opposite of everything they had been told before, and a quite new prospect, and Len saw even Lucinda looking at Mary Johnstone with parted lips and an astonished frown, while Duncan sat solidly staring.

"Now," Mary Johnstone said. "Let me begin to tell you what life is all about."

XXIX

From *The Jottings of G. Berkeley:*

I began these jottings five years ago at the inception of the rocket project. But it is only now, as it begins to work toward its culmination, that I can see it gradually becoming one of the major facts in my life. I begin to wonder what part I have played in it. For the first time, seeing it from Davis City, I begin to wonder what game it is that we are playing.

I did not realize what was happening when Gorlston, the officer from the college where I operated as a history lecturer, came to my floor in the I. O. building.

Betty, my secretary, put her head around my door and looked at the papers on my desk.

"What is it, Betty?"

It was out of the blue. After looking at the papers, she decided she could disturb me. "A Mr. Gorlston."

I had had no further business with Gorlston, and Len Thomas was gone.

"Give me a minute, then show him in."

Something was a little out of line somewhere. I did not think much of it. I try to be accessible, and people try to make use of me.

I wondered if it was something to do with Len Thomas. Gorlston came in looking nervous and hangdog. I did not understand. Until then, I was under the impression that I knew everything.

"Could I have a word with you, Captain Berkeley?" I could not see why he was so ill at ease, when he said it.

"We know one another well enough for you to drop the 'Captain,' Gorlston."

I could see there was something wrong with him.

He sat in my visitor's chair looking at the switch on the desk before him. He obviously knew about those switches "I can only ask you," he said. He looked up at my eyes. Soundlessly, his lips repeated, "I can only ask you."

I looked at him for a moment, then felt beneath the desk. I am not too happy myself about our electronic circuits. He saw it in my eyes. His own went quickly around the room again. "Is there anywhere else we can talk?"

"It would do no good," I told him. In my office, I could at least hope that I had got them all. There would be nowhere else where that would be true, and after what my landlord told me the other week, certainly not my home.

"I don't know how to tell you this."

I am making the attempt to remember exactly the words he used.

"You know. You have interviewed people. It doesn't help to wonder."

It was not himself he was nervous for. I could suddenly see that. He said, "I have a sister in Southeast Territory."

I felt the old twist. Anyone who has relatives, in our business, has hostages to fortune. "Connected with us?"

"Married. To another officer."

I remember I sat looking at him, wondering if he was going to come out with it, and whether I would dig it out, if he made me do it.

"You won't help her by sitting there."

"All right. We have communications by private hand. A messenger."

"You got a letter to show me?"

He shook his head. He had a letter. The microphones were off, but it was not for showing.

He was involving me as well as himself. I should have put the microphone on again, and he knew it and I knew it. Unless I could be quite sure the desk was dead, we were both in trouble. He could see it made me angry.

"Let's go for a walk in the park," he asked me.

"You and I? What excuse do we have?" I told him the facts of life. "If we wanted to be conspicuous, that would be the way to do it, to go out for a private talk, outside this building."

He looked hangdog and despairing.

Suddenly he said, "You told me that these special recruits like Thomas were going to be all right."

I had a dead feeling inside of me. It was there although I could not see what he was getting at. To say Thomas was "all right" was comparative. But he knew what the risks were of the space-shot to Vista, for I had told him. It could not be that.

"You had better tell me what you know, or what you think you know."

He looked up at me. "Southeast Territory produced a candidate. He was the son of P. Vulmany."

"So?"

"I said 'was.' He was chosen as we chose Thomas, but Vulmany withdrew him."

I thought about it. It was out of line. Solicitude for their own offspring, if by some mistake they had them, was not what I would have thought of as a characteristic of our high officials.

"You told me we wanted our best youth," he said. "That it was a privilege and the risks were worth it."

"Even so, it wouldn't be an unnatural action for a doting father. Some parents don't want their sons to take any risks, and no doubt Vulmany wanted his son to stay on this planet with him."

He looked at me as though he wanted to believe me. "You really think so?"

"I'm sure of it. Have you any reason to doubt it?"

"Only that Vulmany didn't appear to mind his son going at first." He touched his pocket, where I did not doubt his letter was. "Like you, he told people in the office that it was an honor and a privilege. Then he happened to have a long talk with C. Q. Lankowitz, on the long-distance scrambler telephone. He turned completely around after that. He not only had his son withdrawn, he had the office burn the record of the fact that he had been selected."

It was ugly. I could see how ugly better than Gorlston did, but I could not tell him that.

"That's nothing. Probably the boy's mother had had time to put a word in. The phone call to Lankowitz was just coincidental."

He looked at me gratefully. "You don't know how it relieves my mind to hear you say that. I wouldn't have liked Thomas to be involved in one of the things we sometimes do, but if you say it's all right, it's all right. I know you liked him too."

I knew then that it was not going to be the only time I would regret telling Gorlston that I liked Len Thomas.

"You go back to the college and don't think of it again. Take my word for it that nothing is going to happen to—what was his name?—Len, if we can help it."

He got up and left me.

I began to walk up and down the office.

P. Vulmany should never have let his son get into it. If he felt like that, he should have known, and stopped it in the early stages. Yet what was I thinking? Making a mountain out of a molehill of gossip told to me by a man like Gorlston? I should never even have listened to Gorlston. What I had been doing was listening to counter-information. I had committed a professional sin by opening up a private line of information inside the office.

XXX

From *The Short History of Arcon*:

When we come to considering the role of the army in the rocket project, we should remember that the army command, and particularly the officers most involved, such as General Koln, Colonel Glasson, and Brigadier Ilallah of the Second Army Swamp Corps, had on their own account a peculiar view of history. It is a view that is not uncommon among army officers and the nobility of almost all human societies on every planet, and the basis of it is a kind of preconception about themselves: the idea that, in some strange way, they, who were most remote from them, nonetheless understood the common people.

It would be interesting, but unhistorical, to explore the

mental background of this odd belief. What we can note is that the view these people took of the ordinary people was, with some slight justification, that they were even simpler versions of themselves. That they shared the same ignorances and the same prejudices, in other words, and were anti-intellectual, having the same distrust of statistics, of science in so far as science exceeded the bounds of engineering and pure mechanics, and of the effect on communities of such difficult concepts as education and the payoff balance. Like the common people, the military minds saw the difficulties and disasters of life arising from the source to which they are always attributed in non-historical comment and lurid fiction, which is to say the machinations of evil men.

It is in this light we must see the General's dispositions of the September 6th and 7th, 506 A. L., for the rocket blast-off, his deployment of the Light Armored Corps near Davis City, and his assembly of the Parachute Regiment in Central Park for what was to be called army games. . . .

XXXI

The Shopping Lists of Mary Jean Smith:

Fillet Steak, all the usual trimmings, for a healthy man?
Imported freshwater bluefish, and something rare?
Wine.

What am I, : widow setting a trap for a younger man? Have I the heart to do it, when he is so good and kind?
He has not seen it, not the death of someone of his own generation, closely connected with him, and he does not know what it is to be so helpless. He does not know how important it is that all associations on this world of ours should always be with someone younger.

XXXII

CORRESPONDENCE FILE

From the Office of
P. Vulmany.
I. O. H. Q.
Eastern Territory.
July 3, 506 A. L.

Dear Son,
I must ask you not to cut yourself off from me. Naturally

the things that have been happening to you have been inexplicable, but you cannot expect me to explain them fully to you, at least by letter.

Believe me, I do know the source of your resentment. It is true that the events you describe were a selection, and it is true that when you were selected I intervened to stop you. But you may well understand that I had my reasons, and when I tell you I do things for your own good, I think that you might consider it possible sometimes that I mean exactly that.

I certainly would not contemplate telling you everything even if I could. It is sufficient to say what I have told you, that the rocket project is not what you think it is, and that from your own point of view, for you to have been involved in it would have been a sheer disaster. As for envying the second man on the list, this Desmond Salford who has gone in place of you, you simply do not know what you are saying. You might as well envy a dying man.

Make an effort to believe me, please. Burn this.

Your far from doting father,
Peter Vulmany.

XXXIII

THE DESERT LIGHT was bright and the air still fresh when Len and Lucinda went out into the space school grounds. It was not only the difference of place, Len thought. It never could be an ordinary morning in anyone's life, the day after they had first heard the Yellow Doctrine.

He and Lucinda were first out of the central building, and they walked out across the parade ground area looking at the training sheds under the walls, and the place where the instructors were waiting for them, out in the open where the tower stood, and the centrifugal and flight-simulator machines. Len thought how things that normally required cover did not need any in that desert atmosphere. When they were away from the building, they turned and looked at the thin spire of the top of the rocket which stood against the blue of the sky above the wall.

It gave Len a different feeling that day, after Mary Johnstone's visit, from the one he had had when they first saw it across the desert, or after the colonel's story. To Lucinda, as they stood looking, he said, "It's strange how a thing like that, a rocket, begins to mean something."

Lucinda too looked at the rocket as though she had to keep some reserve about it, as though it were a thing that was tempting and, at the same time, frightening.

"I suppose, like me, you only knew the Yellow idea partly, but not how wide it was, or how far it went."

"Worse than that," Len confessed. "I thought I did know it, when in fact I didn't know what it was all about."

He had not really understood what it meant before, that a doctrine or a political party should be suppressed. If there was only the opposition propaganda to reconstruct from, you thought you knew, but of course you failed. He noticed that an instructor by one of the training machines was waving to them to come over, but he did not mention that to Lucinda.

Duncan and Penny, who had also come out, came toward them, with Sorensen and Vera following. "We have decided to hold a conference," Duncan said. It sounded natural and inevitable after Mary Johnstone's visit, the more so after a night to think about it. The twenty-four-legged creature that Len had envisaged would want to make up its collective mind. When Sorensen joined them, he said, "The instructors are waving to us."

"They will have to wait," Duncan said, and looked to where Ropotsky and Susan and the rest were coming to join them.

Even after the crash of the aircraft and their talk of escape plans, Len had not quite realized how unified they were becoming, or how impossible it was for an outsider to see it or understand it. After looking around the grounds, Vera pointed in the direction of the swimming pool, which had a concrete apron and bank where they could sit, away from the wall and clear of the instructors, and the whole party moved spontaneously in that direction.

As they seated themselves, the chief instructor came up to them, looking hot after walking right across the grounds. He looked at them indignantly, clearly having no idea what was going on. "You have been allowed out to work," he said. "Maybe you don't understand. The work you do here is essential for your survival."

Len noticed that they waited for Duncan to speak. There was a natural authority about Duncan. It was not what Duncan said, nor did he necessarily consult with them before he said it. Duncan just said what he had said before. "We have decided to hold a conference." When a thing was said by Duncan, it became so solid and rock-hard that even the chief instructor could only stare at it.

"The colonel is not going to allow you to hold conferences," the chief instructor said.

Duncan shook his head. That was obviously the colonel's

business. Meanwhile, they were going to hold a conference.

The chief instructor opened his mouth, closed it, and decided to go off to the main building, presumably to find the colonel.

"Won't they send soldiers to us?" Eliza Teen said.

No one seemed to think that very important, and Lucinda, who had seated herself on the bank by Len, said, "I don't think they'd be that foolish." It was obviously going to be difficult for the authorities to force their bodies into training, or their heads into learning if they did not want to take it, and even if the space school was in a state of paralysis, the colonel would have had to be extraordinarily unwise to make an issue of it immediately.

They turned to the question of the rocket, which they could see above the wall, and what Mary Johnstone had told them the previous night, and whether it was believable or not that the Yellows had somehow taken over the whole rocket venture, including the radio telescope, which they could also partly see above the wall on the hillside. It took a considerable amount of faith to believe that the Yellows intended to fly them out to Vista in what for them would be a year or two, by using up all their fuel and power on the outward journey, and that they were in a position to know that there very likely was a pristine new planet at Vista which they would find inhabitable.

While they sat in the sun and talked about it, Len thought that whoever operated the telescopes would know that Vista had planets, since that could be determined by irregularities of the stellar motion, but not that any were inhabitable. They were obviously going to have to take a number of chances.

"I don't know why they sent a young woman to talk to us and inform us," Ropotsky grumbled. "I would have preferred a man, maybe an astronomer, or someone who could be more technically exact and give us more accurate details."

The group had a tendency to look to Lucinda for the answer to anything like that, just as they looked to Ropotsky himself for matters related to organic chemistry, or to Sorensen to solve physics or engineering problems.

"I don't think that was the idea," Lucinda said. "The way they see it, we don't have any alternative but to go up in the rocket, and if the people who operate the radio telescope and control the flight arrange it so we can't get back, we'll obviously have to make a landing. The reason they sent Mary Johnstone was because of the enthusiastic way she indoctrinated us. The Yellow Party must have decided that we had to be capable of carrying out their aims on another planet."

Len knew what Lucinda meant: to turn them into Yellows. He looked at the water of the swimming pool. But they had been Yellows, or incipient ones, or they would not have been selected.

"As far as we are concerned," Duncan said, looking upward at the sky, "whether we accept the Yellow doctrine will decide if we go in the rocket."

They all looked around at the space school grounds and walls. Beyond them lay the desert. If they did not go in the rocket, the alternative was an escape attempt, which they knew they would have to plan in detail, but which would not necessarily be unsuccessful.

Any soldier knew that it was not the totality of power that mattered, but where it was applied and when. A soldier taken from behind could lose a spray-gun, and another could lose another. Vehicles, aircraft and airport guards were all subject to the same technique of the intense application of local power. But how did they stand with regard to the doctrine that, even if it was suppressed, was still the core of Arcon politics? It was a doctrine more sublime in its range, involving galaxies and stars and the eternity of time, than Len had ever suspected.

"It's a big subject," Salford said. He was looking across the waters of the pool at the space school gate where the sentries stood, and his dark face showed he was still thinking of his escape plans.

"Too big for us?" said Duncan. "When a woman like Mary Johnstone can master it?"

Len was to remember that morning when they discussed Yellow doctrine and recreated it by the pool. Sorensen was the first to say, "I'm for it."

It was all right for him, Len thought. He was a hard-science man, a physicist as well as an engineer. Perhaps it came natural for him to base his personal conduct on a hypothesis that involved the universe, the stars and galaxies, from the cosmos itself down to the structure of the atom.

Sorensen and Vera sat by the pool with the sunlight reflecting from his gold head and her red one. Harold Sorensen's blue eyes looked at them as though it was natural and inevitable to think of the primordial substance of the universe when deciding what to do at a given moment.

"The Yellows see us all as part of a universal process, a building up from the simplest of all things, the gas between the stars," Harold said. "I like that. It's dead against the usual view of the universe, which says it consists of entropy, a running-down, and that everything will be dead in time. Maybe," he admitted, "it's just that I'm a blind optimist."

Duncan looked hard at Sorensen, as though he expected him to go on talking. "That's all you can say to back the Yellows up?" he asked.

Len understood then what Duncan meant by a conference. They were there to give the Yellow doctrine a harder going-over than Mary Johnstone had ever given it. She had given them enthusiasm and emotion and a young woman's drive, but that did not satisfy this group.

Sorensen's eyes became cold blue depths as he looked back at Duncan. "No. It's right. I mean it's physically right," he said. "The gas between the stars consists of the simplest element, pure hydrogen, one proton, one electron. Under the influence of gravity it condenses into the stars. By atomic fusion there, it builds up into helium, iron, and all the complex substances like uranium, with proton and neutron nuclei, and a cloud of electrons like them. The stars blow up and the material is scattered in space again when they reach the nova stage. It forms the planets. There is a power loss. But you are left with material of a higher structure."

Looking at the gold head and blue eyes, Len thought that if you wanted hard reasons, Sorensen could be the kind of man who would give them to you. Duncan looked around their group and along the edge of the pool until he came to Imantha.

"Imantha, you're our chemist. How does that strike you?"

Imantha looked up at Duncan, then glanced at Salford. Salford was looking across the water at the gate in the walls and seemed to be thinking of escape plans. It was not easy for Imantha to go against Salford.

"All right," she said. "You begin to get chemical reactions on planets. When things cool, the building-up process continues in terms of larger molecules. Acid rains washing material down to solvent seas and things like that. When you get lightning and solar radiation in methane and carbon dioxide atmospheres on planets in early stages you get molecules up to organic level."

What are we doing, Len thought, *sitting here talking about galaxies and atoms and molecules?* Surely nothing could be more remote from the problem they had before them.

After she had said her say, Imantha looked at Ropotsky. Everyone knew that Ropotsky was their biochemist.

Ropotsky looked up and looked around at them. He knew what they expected. Like Len he had heard the doctrine that was supposed to make sense of all things.

If it did, Len thought.

"Organic compounds too, on planets," Ropotsky said. "Big molecules pick up new atoms that happen to fit their facets. Once started, they can only build up in a certain order, and when they reach a certain size, they split, and the halves drift off to begin to build again. It's the same building up of higher organisms in biology. The same law applies to living structures, including us. That part of what she said is true, it seems to me. You begin with microscopic specks of life, and gradually run the gamut of all living things until you come to man."

The sun was gradually becoming hotter on the bank and concrete by the pool, and Len saw the whole space crew sitting there turn and look at Ed Creet as though they knew what next was going to happen.

"The human brain is the largest unitary coherent molecular structure in the universe we know so far," Ed Creet said. "A doctrine that connects the universe with us, in fact."

Len remembered his training in communication theory, including cybernetics. Lucinda's dark eyes were on him. "It's not so much its size as its structure," he said. "Its awareness and memory-banks. The state of its organization."

Little Penny had sat so near to Duncan that she was almost in his lap as he lay on one elbow by her. Her eyes were round, with her apparently child-like innocence. She looked around at everyone as though trying to understand them. "As though the universe wanted to think," she said. "It didn't know what it was doing quite, but everything went the same way, until it made us."

It was calm in their part of the space school grounds, and the chief instructor had gone into the central building and had not come out again. Len had continued to look at Lucinda's dark eyes after he had said his word, and she had watched him, asking him if he knew what he was doing, if he was going along with what they were all saying.

"You know this is more like a religion than a political doctrine, don't you?" she said in words that might have been meant for him alone.

Vera looked at Lucinda. Len was not sure what Vera's

specialty was. Considering her looks, it was something, like ecology or paleontology.

"You know it yourself, Lucinda. This isn't an egocentric dogma. The same rules apply to development on any planet. Evolution is bound to progress to maximum, until you get one dominant species that runs out of competition. Man got his maximum fulfillment on the perfect world of Earth. It's just that on Arcon it happened to be the Arcon swamp-frog. Then evolution would stop at that point."

Lucinda had looked away to Vera, and Len was left looking at her profile, seeing that she did know, and was not going to deny what was being said. *Berkeley and his kind chose well*, Len thought grimly. *Choosing the rocket crew for the new planet, they chose our subjects so exactly that our knowledge is almost a trap for us*, he thought.

They had known what they were doing. Mary Johnstone had not needed to shed a Yellow light on them. Her function had only been to put a match to a powder-train.

Salford looked away from the gate and turned his dark face to them. "So you were born to innumerable worlds," he said. "All of them doomed when their suns blow up. A universe of strife and evolution, so some maximum creature can arise on each and reach its own fulfillment. Then what happens? The worlds die, and all that has happened is as though it had never been. All right. Unless. You say it."

Duncan looked at Salford, and then at the company around the pool. The colonel and the chief instructor had come out of the central building by then, and were standing by the space school door, but no one took any notice of them. Duncan said, "All right. Which one of us is going to say it?"

He looked at Susan, their "pure" mathematician, who had not spoken yet.

When he looked, Susan was sitting by Ropotsky and looking at the ground. Then she looked up.

"It only makes sense," she said, "if you assume that the process is going on, and must have a next step. We are creatures that have sense and reason, so why do we assume that the universe hasn't? Or at least some aim, some blind drive, some purpose."

For some reason she looked at Sorensen, who had started it, and whose blond hair was like her own.

"If there is, there's something beautiful about the next step. The whole process is one of selection of structures that are more alive, of a higher form, and more aware.

On a planet, while it lasts, any creature can fulfill its own desires, its animal nature. But the habitable worlds are far apart, and there is no incentive for any creature seeking its own immediate advantage within its lifetime to leave its planet. Why should it? It has grown up perfectly adapted to one world. It has evolved on that world, and it can't find anything better for it on any other."

Susan looked away, at the rocket across the wall.

"But suppose there were some creature so alive and so aware that it could see the universe as a whole and understand the universal purpose. That creature might decide, voluntarily and of its own accord, to fulfill that purpose. The purpose of the universe, you might say, would have become conscious. Because that creature would head outward, seeking new worlds, new evolution and new development. It would be self-selected when it set out. It would suffer selection and survival-of-the-fittest on every new world it came to. When it had learned to survive there, and built a civilization, and not until, it would be self-selected again as it set out for new worlds. Such a creature would populate the universe in time. It would *be* the universe in a form and structure so advanced that we can not imagine. At the time the power of the universe ran out, it would be complete, a cybernetic whole, in one total transformation."

They sat on the bank by the pool in the space school, and Len noticed that the colonel and the chief instructor were coming toward them with a squad of soldiers, but none of them took much notice of that. Duncan was drawing two circles in the dust beside him.

A doctrine, a dogma, Len thought. The Yellow cosmos.

"I want a vote," Duncan said. "You can all find a pebble or some kind of token. Those of you who are for going into the rocket can throw it into this circle here, and those who are against can throw it into the other."

The colonel, the instructor and the squad of soldiers had progressed halfway across the grounds toward them by the time the stones were in.

Looking at the objects in the circle, Len noticed that some of them were coins. Maybe the ones who threw them thought they would have no further use for coins.

Duncan too looked at the answer to his vote, then tossed in two more items for himself and Penny, and then got up. He looked across the pool. "Two of you come with me," he said, and set off around the pool to meet the instructor and the colonel.

Len began to get up, then saw that Sorensen and Ropotsky had already gone. He relaxed again. No doubt Duncan intended to tell the colonel that they were striking for better conditions, or over the food, or for a shade more freedom. He and Lucinda watched the parties meet on the far side of the pool and begin their parley. But they did not worry over negotiations which, though the colonel could not know it, could have only a single outcome.

"I'm glad you voted the same way as I did, Lucinda."

"That's not surprising, since everyone else did."

"It will be all right. As you said before, a Vista world can't be worse than being fugitives in an Arcon swampbog."

On their side of the pool, the couples were talking and watching Colonel Glasson and the instructor, who appeared to be becoming heated. Len watched Lucinda frown, and wondered.

"They have only sent this one young woman to see us," she said.

Len said, "So we might take a few precautions."

Despite all their talk, looking at the sky, he became a little thoughtful.

XXXIV

From *The Jottings of G. Berkeley*:

Looking out of my office window at Davis City, I tried to feel at first as I had, that we were all reliable professional men working together, and that suspicions and gossip that came to me from a man like Gorlston deserved just the check and reassurance I had given him. A city has that effect. I watched people going about their business, and the traffic on the expressway, and I told myself that the very normality of the city meant that there could be nothing wrong at the top.

I spent a lot of time looking out of that window. I myself had prepared the government papers for the desert project. I had attended the Council meeting at which it had been first projected. A space project was what the party had worked for and believed in. It was absurd to think that there was anything wrong with it which I and people similar to myself did not know.

I remembered that, at the Council meeting, I and the Staff had been asked to withdraw while the Delegates considered their decision. Lankowitz, Vulmany and T. Chinn had had meetings since then, which I happened to know. I took the trouble to go through my papers relating to the rocket contracts. I had a considerable amount of material, but none of the key plans showing how the detailed items related together. The key plans were all in Lankowitz' office.

When I thought of what I was going to do, I felt fear.

To ask questions would only draw attention to myself and my suspicions. The alternative was to find out. It took an effort to come to that conclusion. I told myself that I am a coward when acting on my own ideas, and a hero when acting on orders from the leadership, which means they are someone else's.

I was worried about little things, such as that my office light would be seen burning late, high in the darkness above Davis City, and that someone might look up, examine the building as they would have to against the night sky, and say, "Why is he working late; what's he got to keep him?" I was not as worried as I ought to have been about the interior of the building and the people departing along the corridors. When Betty, my secretary, came in, I said, "Look, you might as well go home now." I indicated an innocuous file on my desk and said, "You can't help me with this because it's all Stage Three confidential."

I waited until she had tidied the office before putting on her coat, as she always does. I judged my time to a nicety, and called out, "Betty!"

I could foresee the expression on her face as she opened my door again.

"There is something you can do for me. I shall want to consult the Stage Three index in the Commandant's office. Will you find out for me if there's anyone working late there?"

I knew there would be no one who intended to stay at that hour. C. Q. Lankowitz was out of town, as I had ascertained that afternoon before I took out the Stage Three file. Lt. Mary Johnstone was away at the space project, no doubt telling Len what life was all about. The last thing any of the regular staff would want to do would be stay on when they had a chance to go home early, and there would be no one of high rank to notice if they had an attack of virtue.

I could hear Betty on the phone in the other room. It was only a moment before she came back to me. "Ven Oborin and Cattie Fall were just locking up and setting the selecters. I told them to set them so that your key

100

and mine will open the door and clear the alarms so you can reach the Index."

The internal security of the I. O. building is such that no one can enter the Commandant's section alone. Betty would have to come with me, use her key as well as mine in the door, and stand there watching as I went to the Index to see that I did not trip any of the internal alarms or touch any of the desks or papers. Even that was something that should have been done by Ven Oborin himself or Cattie, but I had guessed they would push it onto my department.

"Look, I am frightfully sorry about this, Betty."

"Could we go now?" She was looking at her watch and I had told her she could go home. "If you only want me to help you to get whatever it is you wanted?"

"I'm sorry, Betty." I indicated the file. "It may take me up to two hours to discover just what it is I do want."

She stood on one leg and looked bleak. She would sit in her outer office doing nothing for two hours that might easily become three, and not get home till midnight.

"I don't want to suggest that you leave me your key," I said.

She would be breaking every rule of the I. O. internal security system by doing that.

"Unless you want me to come to your apartment and drop it later," I said. I watched her eyes. She knew what I was suggesting, and what it would mean if I called at her place at that hour.

Silently, she took the key out of her bag and laid it on my desk.

For an hour after she had gone, I sat there horrified, looking at that key. It was my chance to reach C. Q. Lankowitz' desk, and I would never get the chance again.

I could not believe that it was I, an experienced operator, who was nervous as I left my office. Things that I would do anywhere else looked like incredible risks when applied against our own organization. I took elaborate precautions that no one should see me in the corridor. I was afraid they would read my intentions on my face. At the same time, I told myself that it was only superstition, my fear of the electronic eyes that watched me. I was careful to break each ray-beam twice as I went past it. The record-trace in the morning would show that two persons had gone from my office right up to the door of the department.

As I used both keys, I blocked both eye-beams with my back. Inside, the real risk began. I could not close the door and I dare not leave it wide open, so I used a letter file to partly jam it. I opened the Index file first, so that if the alarm went off I had my cover story. Then I turned my attention to the desk. Not often before had I so felt my lack of knowledge of electronic theory. The switches for opening the inner doors are normally controlled by a remote computer. I was sweating when I pushed the slip of rubber between the last set of contacts, and the door swung open.

I had carefully examined C. Q. Lankowitz' office every time I had been in it. I believed I knew the location of at least fifty percent of the electronic eyes. That was when I needed the time, to advance by inches, using my ray detector. No one could do that kind of work unless they had been trained in it by ourselves. I had to stand motionless when I reached the desk and memorize the exact sequence of switches I had seen Lankowitz use the last time I had stood before it. It was only just in time that I remembered a movement he had made shifting his weight in his chair. I had to work my way around the desk to reach it.

Sitting in his chair, I had to consider every movement of my hands and feet. When I had the rocket plans before me I could hardly read them.

I just sat looking, knowing that it would take me at least a quarter of an hour to get out of that room again. I had always known that our higher leadership sometimes had to do things that would not be understood by the ranks below them. But not that, I thought. Not that.

Looking at the rocket plans, it seemed to me that I was seeing the end of all things.

XXXV

From the diary of J. Adolf Koln:

Aug. 17, 506 A. L.
A man is nothing.
The man is there, his flesh and blood, his sinew and his judgment. It is not what he is. It is what he will do with himself, and whether he will back his judgment, completely, and in a single cast of fortune.
As I am doing in the so-called army games to be held in Central Park on the 7th.

Aug. 21, 506 A. L.
The army has every reason to be there in force. It is the assembly of the people I am thinking of, and the

fatal confusion if the event were to coincide with disor-
ganization of the morning or lunchtime rush hour. Yet
if I am too late the Senate will be in session. I must give
great thought to timing.

Aug. 25, 506 A. L.

Every possible reaction of the politicians must be
thought out in advance. The temptation to disrupt the
telephone services is great but must be resisted. How
the people will behave when they know the truth is
something we must feel by instinct. The army will ap-
pear to be present by accident and, from then on, every-
thing must be governed by the press releases. I do not
think there is one chance in a hundred that the public
will not respond with some kind of riot. If possible, the
politicians themselves must be persuaded to give the
order to bring the troops in. We must be in control, and
in a position to act, without any appearance at all of
having sought it. I must appear fumbling and dilatory,
unwilling to comply with popular demand on the grounds
of a reluctance to break legality. Then I must seem
abrupt and decisive, and appear on the public screens
at the same time as I arrest the Senators.

Aug. 27, 506 A. L.

I slept badly last night, and this is bad. It is not the
kind of thing an effective general should do on the
approaching eve of a major battle.

I have to think and feel my way into the situation, and
take account of any little thing that might go wrong. It
is right that I should worry about detail, but I must not
let it distract me from the main event, from its physical
actuality and its visual and emotional impact. The space
crew as they emerge, for example, must get a public
showing. It is inevitable that they will be bewildered,
and that will look like guilt. It will be up to Intelligence
whether they present them individually, allow them to
be interviewed and have "case histories" presented, or
whether they just lump them together as "political and
Information Office nominees," with implications of effete-
ness, privileged choice, and nepotism.

But the central event, I am quite sure, must be the
main thing. As I see it, it will come like a bolt from the
blue, literally, in the Arcon sky, bursting upon the peace-
ful life of the city. Fear is bound to be the first impulse,
and that is what I will call the time of disorganization,

to be succeeded rapidly by curiosity, relief, amazement, and then, what we must carefully foster, the tide of anger against the politicians. It will not be for what they have done, though the thing will be visible enough and actual enough to cause a surge of outrage. It will be the fact that they, the known people in the Senate, knew about it, planned it, executed it, and that they, the supposed "friends of the people," kept it entirely to themselves and did not say. Why should they do that? It is that which will display the hollowness, the mockery, that never, in their public speeches, did they once confide to the public that it was even possible to do it. That then is the psychological moment when our men must go out onto the streets and put it to the crowd that they could go out into space, their own sons and daughters maybe, while we could not.

It will only take a single incident then, a group of Information Office men protecting Senators, from around whom we can withdraw our screen at a crucial moment, who can be persuaded to fire into the crowd in their own defense, to turn the outrage, the questions, to a deeper sense of a gross betrayal.

Aug. 31, 506 A. L.

As the time draws nearer, only one week to go now, I find I am more serene. I no longer wonder or worry so much about the details of what will happen, and my mind goes more to afterward, to the sense of national identity and euphoria that always succeeds revolution or any new thing, even if it should be seen, in the immediacy of history, as a great disaster.

That will be the time when we must make it clear that we have not caused the disaster, but have responded to it. We must be seen not as the usurpers of power, but as those who have cleared a way through corrupt power to make room for new things. It will depend on the people's will, we must say in statements of the utmost gravity, whether we turn to space or solve Arcon's problems. Since we are sure of the answer, knowing the people as we do, I truly believe that we can give them a sense of participation by holding a referendum. In time, when the time comes, though not now for they are rightly concerned with details, I must talk to Glasson and Lomax about this, and about how we can give the people a sense of blood-brotherhood, and land, and national purpose.

I think a uniform for everyone, at least for the men, would be a good idea. Nothing unites people more than an identity of dress. To put women into uniform is more difficult, but I think mistakes have been made about that in the past in the way it has been done. Short skirts, and an emphasis on sex beyond the present fashion, would be the way to do it, so that those in uniform would look younger, more daring, the forward-looking kind. But it would be important not to overdo this. Maximum provocation would be combined with the most rigid moral code. Those who fail to live up to the precepts might be subjected to some kind of public lashing.

Drama, in that way, and the sense of danger, and of the meaning of what people do, could be maintained in public life. The public lashing of a naked woman should not take place more often than once every year or two, at least to any grave extent, while public executions of men should take place more abruptly, never when there is the slightest doubt about the case, and, say, every twelve months. It is vital to make people think that the things they do have meaning, but that the bad things only happen to other people, who are definitely bad, not like themselves, so that the distinction of what we are remains, and we can see ourselves marching, six deep, in a column with flags, into an ordered future.

I am sure that this, the certainty of a fixed system, is the way to bring happiness to our Arcon people, and that to bring the space rocket down, to its startling public landing in Central Park in Davis City, with all the political questions which that will raise, is the way to expose the corruption of this planet, and so the way to do it.

XXXVI

CORRESPONDENCE FILE

Post 43121 R
Space School,
Project J.
North Arcon.
Sept. 1, 506 A. L.

To the Office of the Commandant,
I. O. H. Q.
Davis City.
By I. O. Messenger.

Dear Commandant Lankowitz,

This will probably be my last report on the training of the space crew, as blast-off is now definitely scheduled for five days' time.

As I told you in my last report, we have had singularly little trouble with the crew since the briefing given to them by Lieutenant Johnstone, and, as I forecast, this state of affairs has continued with only minor lapses. The young man Desmond Salford, whom I understand was a substitute, has shown signs of temperament, and this is perhaps understandable. Less understandable has been a lapse by the electronics man, Len Thomas, who caused a short-circuit in the electronics room by an act of inadvertence that would certainly have been fatal to him had it happened in the rocket. A certain amount of equipment was destroyed. The man Duncan has now been officially confirmed as captain, and his behavior has proved exemplary.

I must compliment whoever thought of sending an outside officer to give the briefing, and an enthusiastic young woman at that. Not only did it prove more impressive than if it had come from any of the regular staff here, but by maintaining our cover as instructors, we have been able to sustain our apparent ignorance of certain matters, and to avoid answering awkward questions.

In answer to your queries, the "genuine" method of selection of the space crew, whereby the officers engaged in the selection were allowed to believe in what they were doing, does not appear to have had any ill effects. It is true that, immediately following Mary Johnstone's visit, as my report of that time told you, there was a certain recalcitrance. The shock of hearing the Yellow doctrine expounded by such an earnest young woman must have had an effect on them. It is natural, I presume, that they should ask themselves if it was genuine. But you will understand that in view of my position here, I cannot really answer your further questions. I feel inhuman enough as it is, and I cannot allow my feelings to become involved.

Yours respectfully,
W. Pintopler,
Captain.
(Chief Instructor)

XXXVII

Military Intelligence Report:

Forwarded from the
Office of Colonel Glasson.
BQ/TPM/38239 - Z.

For the information of
General Koln exclusively.

Approach to the interior workings of the telecommunications building operating the radio telescope has been extremely difficult. The Information Office screen has been exceptional. I attribute the death of 38107 - Z to this cause, though I have found no trace of him. A grave could well be dug in the sand here within yards of the telecommunications building.

I am, however, able to reassure you about certain features.

(1) The rocket, following blast-off, will be under direct control from the building here.

(2) There are, as you are aware, other radio telescopes operating around the planet, which will maintain twenty-four hour coverage, but these are linked electronically through the building, and the space capsule will not be out of control at any time.

(3) There is no way the rocket can escape control until a final signal is sent to it, consisting of a short burst of code, through the most powerful radio telescope, and this will not be done until the capsule is approaching Vista.

(4) I have been assured by the Chief Operator himself, unaware he was talking under the influence of a hypnotic drug, that the rocket can be placed within yards of any prescribed point in our solar system.

38239 - Z.

XXXVIII

From *The Jottings of G. Berkeley*:

I sat with the plans before me. How could it be? Even then, looking with horror, I could not understand it, though I have seen the things that men can do in my time.

With my finger, I traced the lines of the blueprint inside

the outer shell. They would not see it, because of the casing that would conceal the space vehicle and the upper part of the rocket until it was in space. As it stood before blast-off, the space capsule and the upper effective parts would be concealed, by the sheathing and the protective nose cone which would be shed when it left the atmosphere. Only then would they have a chance to learn and know, too late, what kind of vehicle it was in which they were riding.

I did not accept it at once when I checked the blueprints. I went over it again, reading the plans carefully as I mentally checked off each item. There was the first stage, the big chemical rocket that would lift them into the upper atmosphere, and the second stage that would carry them into space again. The atomic ion-drive stage would come into action then, and above it was the space capsule containing the living quarters. There was nothing between those two items, and I did not have the technical knowledge to check the specifications of the atomic units, or to decide whether they were adequate for the task assigned to them, but I began to suspect a little.

XXXIX

WHEN THE DAY of the blast-off dawned, Len got out of bed in his room and went to the window. The first sun was just coming up over the eastern hill and the shadows were long across the space school grounds below him, and he thought about their time in the space school, and how long it had seemed while it was happening, and what a short and inadequate training it seemed now that it was finished.

Whatever it had been, it was over now, and this was likely to be the last dawn he would see on Arcon, for today was the day they set off for Vista. He turned to look at the new clothes, comprising a silver, tight-fitting suit, which had been laid out for him, and he thought about it and wondered if they had been right to accept the voyage to Vista the way they had.

It was certain that they would not have accepted it, if all they had heard was the colonel's story of a spy-flight and a journey that would take them more than a lifetime to go out and back to Vista. He glanced out of the window again, at the space school walls. He did not know how they would have broken out, but he was sure they would have someway. The twenty-four-legged beast was capable of decision, and it was capable of dying. But then the Yellow girl had arrived, to tell them not only what the voyage truly was, but what life was all about. He wondered how much their ultimate decision had been affected by Lucinda's point, by the way she had pointed out that even if they did escape, and were free on Arcon, the only life they could expect there was that of fugitives, outlaws in one of the farther swamp-lands.

Better to go to Vista, to perform one heroic act, than that. But that had not been it. Standing alone and naked in his room, looking out at the dawn before he dressed, Len thought that it was at the same time the madness, and the beauty and logic of the Yellow dream, that had done it.

They were right, he thought. *Whoever selected us was right. It is just the mad kind of thing we would do.* And a beatific grin broke out on his face, occasioned at least in part by the thought that this was the day when he and Lucinda would at least be free to be alone together in one of the tiny cabins that would be their accommodation in the rocket.

They were right in choosing us, he thought as he turned to dress, *because we are just the kind of fools who would believe it.* And he added a rider to that as he stood before his window and pulled on his support-suit tights. *We are the kind of people who would believe it whether it was true or not,* he thought, and, despite the apprehension that was inevitable on a day which was virtually a blast-off and marriage in one, he looked upward, grinning.

Breakfast on that day was one of those awkward times. "So that is the last time we sleep in our separate rooms," Penny said, smiling with apparent innocence at Imantha across the table in the space school diner.

Imantha was one of those who was looking with visible apprehension at the prospect of being shot off into space and effectively married off, both on the same day. It had been all right to come to a decision about it some weeks ago, when the alternative had been to encourage Salford to make plans for them to fight their way out across a thousand miles of desert, but that morning was not looking so good to Imantha.

Maybe that was because she was Salford's girl, Len thought. He too, if he had been faced with the prospect of being shut up with Salford in a spaceship cabin for an indefinite period, would have been apprehensive.

A soldier came down the line dealing out the regular fruit juice and saying, "You are advised to have a light breakfast this morning." Perhaps life was different for a girl, Len thought.

Lucinda, who looked pale but composed, said, "There is no reason why any two girls or two men who wish should not share one of those rocket cabins we saw when they took us there for rehearsal."

The soldier was still in earshot, so she too had to sound innocent about it when she spoke of their one and only highly-organized visit to the rocket a few days earlier. Ropotsky, who was passionately in love with Susan, looked at Lucinda as though she had gone mad. Len, for his own good reasons, just wished Lucinda would not refer at all to their rehearsal departure from the space school, which had been complicated from his point of view by certain matters.

After all, he thought, they only had Mary Johnstone's word for it about the preparations the Information Office was allegedly making at the radio telescope to give them a quick journey and the ability to land at Vista, while the colonel had told them from the first something entirely different.

When the soldier went away, he hissed, "Lucinda!"

"If anyone wants to make an arrangement to share a cabin with someone of their own sex when we are free to do as we like," Ropotsky said, "he can count me and Susan out."

"I haven't forgotten," Lucinda said to Len, looking at him in a composed way, and as though she could with difficulty, deal with other things too, as well as having her love-life complicated by rocket travel.

"Don't," Len pleaded, looking at the somewhat fish-like and in some cases startling appearance of everyone along the table. "Because of these suits we knew we would have to wear today, I went to an enormous amount of trouble."

Duncan, who took the cabin arrangements he had made with Penny as completely obvious and no one's business, frowned. "Everyone will cooperate, Len, but it will be completely unnecessary," he said.

"I'm for Len," Salford said. "I don't trust anybody."

"I'm sure Mary Johnstone was genuine," Ropotsky said. He looked out of the window, where the blue early-morning sky showed no sign of a cloud that might delay the blast-off, then got up from the table. "Anyway, it's too late to do anything else now, isn't it?"

110

It was quite a ceremony on the parade ground, with both suns up over the hill, the shadows starting to shorten, a line of trucks drawn up, and about a hundred men in front of the truck facing their little fish-suited line of twelve.

Colonel Glasson walked between the opposing lines and addressed them. While he talked, Len looked past him at the space school gate, which stood open that day, and wondered if history would have been different if it had been kept open earlier. *Suppose we could have just walked out*, Len thought.

"Your training has covered everything you have to do," Colonel Glasson said, facing the space crew with the guard of honor behind him. "I don't have to tell you now about taking up your stations in the rocket well before blast-off time. Your success is up to you. Blast-off is automatic, and you will be under radio control until halfway to Vista, so you can't do that wrong. There will be some maneuvering of your space vehicle by the radio telescope before you are put on a course for Vista, and you must expect that. We wish you good luck. May you have a happy life in your rocket, and your children will no doubt consecrate a monument to you when they get back to Arcon. Farewell. Dismiss."

As a speech, they found it barely adequate.

They talked about his suggestion of unexpected maneuvers as they went across the dust of the parade ground to the waiting trucks. "There shouldn't be anything like that," Ed Creet said. "Every single thing that's going to happen should all have been done and rehearsed beforehand."

It was only a chance conversation as they mingled and broke ranks and crossed to their girls to get in the separate trucks with them. The soldiers were to ride with them, and it was no surprise that they were held to an exact schedule for their ride down to the rocket, and were under heavy guard on that day.

"I told you it was a mistake," Salford said.

"It's as well Len is taking a few precautions," Ropotsky said.

Len said, "Shut up."

The space school wall slipped back, and because of the plume of dust the convoy was kicking up, it looked as though they were descending the hillside on the trail to the rocket at dizzy speed. Len watched the rocket growing and beginning to reach up into the sky as they came down toward it. There was not much to see. Outwardly, and with its sheathing still on, it looked like a series of long, smooth-faced cylinders. The difference was that this time there was a feather of vapor from one of the higher vents, and fewer men and transports around the base of it. Lucinda sat down in the truck and looked at the soldiers who rode with them.

"I saw it when they brought us down before for rehearsal," she said when Len sat down with her. "It looks about as beautiful as an oil-rig."

When they left the trucks under the big concrete wall of the launching pad and were walking the fifty yards to the wire-cage elevator that ran up the gantry to the platform and gangway to the space capsule entry, Lucinda fell. It was those half-buried pipes, which, along with the fuel valves and wheels and conduits, all part of the control system, made the rocket site look untidy. The soldiers had been standing back, letting them walk to the rocket in their own way, but some of them went at once to help Lucinda. The party split. One half went on toward the elevator cage beneath the gantry. Salford and Duncan chose that moment to wander off to look at some item of equipment. Soldiers at once started after them, and the sergeant began to call those who had gone on ahead to come back. His orders were to keep the party together. For about ten seconds Len was out of sight behind a wheel-valve and a transformer stage where the lines came in from the distant bunkers. The returning half of the party picked him up on the way back and he was right in the middle of them from the moment he was in view from behind the transformer housing.

Smooth.

Lucinda was on her feet again and looking down at her leg. "You can't hold up a rocket because a girl has twisted her ankle." She had unfastened one of the side-zips down her hip and thigh, and the flesh was showing. The soldiers were looking at it. Lucinda's eyes were flickering around, noting the exact position of everyone. It was only a few tiny items that were being passed from hand to hand anyway, from Len.

He had decided to move the stuff down to the rocket at rehearsal. Even in the girls' suits it would have been hard to conceal anything from the soldiers in the trucks. It had been a risk. He had had enough trouble causing loss and damage in the school electronics laboratory anyway.

112

The party, moving together, and with Lucinda limping, moved on in a more crowded way. They were supposed to move separately, with plenty of air and view all around them, but they had to help Lucinda.

"It isn't going to do much good anyway," Len said when the first six of them were in the cage and traveling up the gantry, watching the diagonals of its skeleton frame go by.

"What do you want it for?" Ropotsky asked.

"I just get nervous when other people do things."

As they went upward in the elevator, the mountains around the valley sides seemed to shrink, and the more distant peaks came up behind them. They were high in the air when they reached the gantry platform, about four hundred feet. The guards who had been stationed up there to see that they got in the rocket were looking over the edge. "What was the holdup down there?" one said, coming toward them suspiciously as the cage arrived and they stepped out.

"Is that the gangway we have to cross?" little Penny said, pointing. "That settles it. I'm not going. I'd rather die than cross that." She went back into the cage again, and had to be dragged out. Penny was not carrying anything, and Duncan, who was, could not help her. It had been decided that Penny was too small to conceal anything, even a small transistor.

This should have been a poignant and dramatic moment, Len thought, looking out over the view from the rocket gantry platform. The horizon was hazy in the direction of Davis City. Lucinda, coming close to him and looking in that direction too, said, "I suppose it is our last view of Arcon."

"We don't aim to interfere with that," Len said. "In fact it's far too late now, and I don't think we can interfere with anything." And they went on, across the gangway.

In the distance, they could see a car driving away from them across the desert as they went in through the circular door. The sensation of dizzy height stopped across the threshold, and they might as well have been in a skyscraper, instead of in the nose of a four-hundred-foot rocket except that the machine-deck where they came in was full of pipes and plumbing and the big cylinders of Ropotsky's bio-tanks with their air and fluid pumps. With a metal spiral staircase leading up through the center to the two

113

higher decks in the crew capsule, the spaceship had something of the appearance of the interior of a submarine.

There was a period of waiting while the second party came up in the elevator and across the gangway, so they stood in the doorway and looked out at the wastes of Arcon. "Did I do well?" Penny said. "They've forgotten something. They should have married us all before we left, by the marriage rites of Arcon."

"We'll get married according to the Vista rites," Duncan said. "When we have decided what they are."

"This is a psycho-social matter," Lucinda said. "Duncan can marry all the other couples when we are in space, except Penny and himself. They are the two who will have to stay unmarried."

"To hell with that," Duncan said. "If I can't get married, the rest of you will have to manage as best you can without it."

Sorensen came in last, and stood by the door and looked at Duncan. Duncan nodded, and Sorensen operated the hydraulic lever, so that the circular door began to close, cutting off the view of Arcon. As they watched, the circle became a crescent, and the crescent became an arc. At first they could see the men on the gantry platform operating wheels and pulling levers, and the gangway they had crossed was lifting and tilting as it swung away from the rocket's side, then that view was lost to them and they could only see the sky and the car far away in the desert, still heading away from them and the rocket and pulling its little plume of dust behind it. That too was lost then, and with it the daylight, so that they were left in the rocket's own interior artificial lighting with the bio-tanks and the pumps of the machine-deck.

It was different then, with them turning a little oddly to stand and look at one another on the metal deck, surrounded by the metal walls. The air, which they had noticed when they came in, had a slightly artificial oil-and-machine smell, but they would get used to that soon, Len thought, and that would seem like normal air. Some of them moved, and began to ascend the spiral stairway, to the higher cabin-deck and the control dome in the nose of the rocket, at present covered by protective sheathing, where Duncan and Salford and Susan and Len had their blast-off stations and blast-off couches, but Len turned and found Lucinda beside him, and put his arm around her.

They kissed for a moment before they went up the

114

spiral stair to the higher decks, and there was some of that going on too among the other couples. "Come," Len said, taking Lucinda to the spiral stair. "Let's go and choose our cabin—even if they are all identical."

XL

From *The Jottings of G. Berkeley*:

I felt the need to kill.

It seemed entirely logical and reasonable that I should decide to murder C. Q. Lankowitz that night, as I sat at his desk looking at the rocket plans. It was not so much a decision. It was just something that emerged out of the whole of my life as I had lived it.

I found myself looking back over the fifteen years I had worked in the Information Office to the time when, beginning to express Yellow opinions to my young friends in Davis City, I had been "investigated" by the Information Office, arrested, taken down to the cells, interrogated, and eventually recruited. I wondered if there were any other Yellows like C. Q. Lankowitz in our office who, like Lankowitz had to be, were just a fraud. I knew that I dared not stay too long in his office, but I made sure before I left that the rocket project was just a trick that he had perpetrated on us.

Maybe things were like that, I thought as I began to use my ray-detector and work my way back to the door and the outer office. Maybe it was inevitable that the leadership of an organization like the Yellow Party should be twisted, but that did not mean that genuine workers like myself were going to stand for it when we discovered how we had been misled. It was not just the twelve young people who were due to fly in the thing, though I knew I was too late to save Len Thomas. It was the party.

Or *was* I too late to save Len Thomas? I saw Lankowitz' secretary's engagement notebook on her desk, and the idea that I might still do something, perhaps even stop the rocket, was the first weakening of my purpose. My clear mind became confused. It was no longer a simple matter of me and Lankowitz and what was good for Arcon. I began to think of time, and all the time from then on, when I left Lankowitz' office, then my office, and then the Information Office building to cross the city, I was thinking and counting the hours I had left, in which to stop the rocket.

I had to discover if it was possible first, and the secretary's notebook was the clue to that. It depended if he had any appointments scheduled for the following morning. I worked my way to her desk, and opened the book, and saw he had a full list of engagements for the sixth, starting at nine A.M. That meant he would almost certainly be back at his flat in Parkland Towers at some hour that night. I felt the spray-gun in my armpit holster and knew, or rather believed, that I had no alternative after that but to threaten him and force him to stop the rocket. I was not sure, but I believed that he could do it on some pretext or another by one telephone call to the desert outpost. It seemed perfectly clear to me that the only course open to me was to go to Parkland Towers and make him do it.

I was surprised at my certainty as I left his office and walked down the interior corridors along which I had come with such doubt and trepidation little more than an hour before. But then I had only suspected, and feared that I was suspecting our leader unworthily. Now I knew. All of us were responsible for some part of the rocket project, but he was responsible for the whole, for putting the parts together. It did cross my mind that what I should do was call a party Council to emergency session, and accuse Lankowitz and put my case, but I could not even act on that until the next day, and even if, by assembling a few loyal men such as Gorlston, I put Lankowitz under arrest in the meantime by a kind of palace revolution, it would take up to five days to assemble the delegates, and by then the rocket would be well on its way to Vista.

I do not know if I actually doubted whether the Council would stop the rocket after it had been sent off. My mind slid over that and the question of whether their actions would be determined by humanitarian considerations or policy. I just went to my own office, closed up everything and put things to rights in the normal way, and then went down through the building and took my car to cross the city. As I went out into the night at nearly midnight what I was going to do seemed quite clear to me once again.

Facing the first city lights and the sparse traffic, I told myself it was not the first time that an Information Office man, even an agent, though not usually a captain, had gone out into the city either to kill someone or force him to do something he did not wish to do. There were stories in the past of sudden deaths of leading members of the hierarchy, and though I had thought, as everyone does, that that kind of thing did not belong to my generation, I now saw that it did belong, as much as to any others. It was a matter of purification, I told myself. Any authoritarian organization is like that. When the leadership becomes too sophisticated and begins to play with the essentail and vital matters of party aims as though they too were toys, then force and assassination were the cleansing weapons.

Crossing the city and seeing the lights of night-town below me as I traveled the dark expressway, I told myself I was thinking entirely in party terms. I was not concerned with the actual actions. I knew that Lankowitz, in the penthouse flat that the Information Office provided for him, did not live alone. There was the bodyguard-servant with whom he was also provided, as part of his commandant's prerequisites while in the city, but I, or any competent operator, could deal with him.

What I did not quite realize I was doing, was going man-to-man to confront C. Q. Lankowitz.

It began well enough. When I came down from the dark expressway, it was into the quiet, creekside midnight of the city's best residential area. I took an operator's natural precautions, stopping at B-block and walking the remaining distance. I entered C-block without being seen from the private gardens, and took the private elevator—not the public one—to the select upper floors. I was in the corridor on the landing where his door was, seeing the view of the city lights from the window and wondering how it would look from his roof garden, before I found the need to determine my actions more precisely.

A feeling swept over me then, but I conquered it.

When I rang at his door, I turned away and stood a little sideways. I had to watch the landing and, at the same time, if his servant answered the door, it was important that I should take him before he recognized me, since I did not want to have to kill him. When the door opened, I swung around with my gun in my right hand and my left arm up across my face. The man who faced me at the door was Lankowitz.

We went in. From the start, he could have had no illusions about my intentions, and I asked him about the servant. He told me that since he had been out of town he had given the man leave of absence. Once the outer door was closed, I opened other doors and made sure that he was not lying. He was perfectly composed. He went ahead of me into the living room, with me pushing doors open as I went, and he stood in the middle of the room, indicated a chair, and said, "Would you like to sit down a little?" I caught an expression on his face which was not fear, but something more like interest.

I decided that that room was bugged. It was what I would do in Lankowitz' position, especially if I were playing a critical game for high stakes. I would not let him touch anything or sit down in the room where he evidently wished to stay. "We will go out onto your roof garden," I said. I watched him, but he only looked at me again with that look of interest.

"What do you want, Berkeley?" he said as he led the way. "I assume this is a private matter?"

"We will arrange for you to stop the rocket."

He showed no emotion of understanding my intentions.

"Ah," he said. "Your homosexual attraction to that young man, Len Thomas. I had a report about that."

We were in the roof garden, which I did not know. There was a seat there, illuminated from the windows and by the parapet that lay beyond it. I would not let him sit on the seat since there might be a button concealed there somewhere that he could press. I motioned him to the parapet, resisting the desire to press the trigger or attack him physically as he went to it. I sat on the seat myself.

There was no homosexual relationship between myself and Len Thomas. It was a figment of Gorlston's mind. Yet such is the paperwork in the office that the suggestion had only to appear and he had got a report on it.

"I am disappointed in you, Berkeley," he said, sitting down a little sideways on the parapet, with the city lights behind him. "Do you know I had a bad report on you from Pilsen? I took leave to disagree with it. Your work preparing the government papers for the rocket project was first class. I had my eye on you for the highest office. Our shortage of men with grasp and vision is such that I had even mentally placed you as my successor."

He took my breath away by the effrontery of his flattery in this situation. It was incredible that he should expect me to believe what he was saying, yet he said it in the calmest voice. I had only to press the trigger of the gun I held in my lap, with the spray-catch set at its lowest charge, to send him tumbling into the dark depths as his body stiffened. I could get away with it, too. When his body was found, the tiny mark on the skin that was all that would show would be lost in his massive injuries. No one would know how he came to fall from his roof garden at a time when he was alone.

"Your loss of power in the party may be sooner than you think, Lankowitz." My voice sharpened as I said it. "For five hundred years our people have worked for the day when men could move on and leave this planet, and now the opportunity has come, and what have you given us? A fraud."

I could see him examining my face in the half-light with what looked like curiosity as much as calm intentness.

"Are you really interested, Berkeley, in what we might call the less personal aspects?"

"Yes!" Without knowing why, I pointed the gun at him in an almost unconscious movement.

He slowly drew a breath. I believe he must have known how near he was to death at that point.

"There never was a chance," he told me after a moment when he must have discovered that he was still alive. "You have one disadvantage in this business, Berkeley—that you have never met General Koln. In the first interview I had with him I saw the kind of man he was. He arranged a trap for us, the only way he could demonstrate that the Information Office was run by Yellows."

I sat there not thinking, not believing, not even trying to understand it.

How could I believe that Koln, whom I had heard of only as a crude and aggressive general, born in the provinces and not even properly acquainted with the capital, would have the cunning to make use of us?

"You might have underestimated him, but I don't think you would," he said. "You would have realized as I did that you just could not place him as the kind of army man who would intrigue and plan, and invent an unlikely enemy for Arcon, and a rocket project, just to increase the army estimates. It was the kind of intrigue involving so much work and duplicity for so little, that only a very sophisticated person would undertake it. And his whole approach showed he was not that kind of man at all."

I sat looking past Lankowitz at the city lights. In my field of view I could see him picked out in silhouette against the lights. Without even looking at him, I could see if he made the slightest move.

"You are telling me you did this for General Koln?" I said. "Let's look at it, Lankowitz. Our party has been striving to send man into space again for five hundred years. By chance, because of an intriguing general, we get the opportunity to make a space-shot. Now, I don't know what plans you think General Koln has. But this isn't a little thing for the party. Our whole aim is bound up in it. You can't pretend to have a space project, revitalize the party, rouse their enthusiasm by making them think we have achieved our aims at last, and then reveal it was just an intrigue, a fraud, to deceive an army general. If you do, the disillusion will sicken all our own ranks. You will destroy the party."

We were sitting looking not so much at one another as past one another, I at the city and he at the night behind me, and taking a little time about the things we said. I heard my own voice talking and wondered why it sounded as it did, moralizing and platitudinous, so that it was apparent that I was a man of only the middle rank, talking to C. Q. Lankowitz.

"Is that it, Berkeley?" he asked me quietly. "Is that why you've come here?"

He was a man who dealt with and could be expected to face the naked truth. I gave it to him.

"No. If it were that, I would not have come here. I would have called the party Council. Maybe it is personal. I've been looking at your rocket plans, Lankowitz. The true ones, in your desk."

He made a sound like a sigh of understanding.

"How much are you prepared to do for policy, Lankowitz?" My voice strained as I tried to keep it down, when I had to say it. "Twelve of our best people. Young people. In a rocket that can go nowhere. That has not the power to go anywhere." I had to wait a moment before I could say the rest of it.

He said it for me.

"And that can't be landed."

XLI

The Shopping Lists of Mary Jean Smith:

What have I got to complain of, when for a long time now I have known such happiness as there is to be found on Arcon?

The blue dress.
First examine what it reveals of the bones below the neck. He must not know.
Shoes.
Bag.

It must just look as though I have bought a
new outfit, not a dress to fit my shrinking body.
Dinner—cold.
Remember that I am liable to make mistakes in
cooking.
Drinks. Fruits. Nuts.

The cyanide rat poison.

XLII

From *The Jottings of G. Berkeley*:

He knew he was taking a risk when he sat calmly on
the parapet and told me that the rocket could not be
landed. He talked as though I would discuss it reasonably.

"Let's be careful about this," he said. "What happens if
you stop the rocket and expose it for what it is? That is
the one way you will destroy the party. You must understand that. Contrary to what you said, if the rocket goes
up and looks as though it is behaving normally, then no
one will be the wiser. The party will believe we have made
a successful space-shot, and will be willing to try again.
It will be exactly the boost we need. It is your way, not
mine, that will result in disillusion and tear us apart with
internal factions."

I sat looking at his silhouette against the city lights with
a sinking feeling. He was monstrous. He was inhuman.
And yet how clear he was. There is something awful about
it, when once in your life you find you are facing the
clarity of a greater intellect. I just began to understand
what it was to try to talk and argue with C. Q. Lankowitz.

I should have shot him. I should not have given him the
chance to say a word, but I could not stop the rocket that
way. "You can't mean you did this deliberately?" I said.

His face in the half-light examined me.

"Pilsen warned me of your weakness, Berkeley. They
are good faults—idealism and a tendency to think in too
simple terms. People acquire sublety and balance by experience. What I saw you had was the good heart, the
loyalty, the drive. Those things are irreplaceable."

He was sitting in judgment on me.

I had the gun, yet he judged. He was right in what he
said of me.

It was as though during all my life in Arcon I had been
talking to people who were unsophisticated, of a simple

kind, while C. Q. Lankowitz was a man who saw everything objectively and from a great height. He was on a different level, a level I might attain to, but only if he was there to teach me.

"You are talking about people's hearts being in the right place when you are sending twelve young people to their deaths?" I said. Even then, I could not believe it.

I could see him watching me, just silently asking me if it worried me if twelve strangers died. More people than that died in Davis City every hour or two, and neither I nor he nor anyone ever gave a thought to it.

"It's Len Thomas, isn't it?"

"If there is Len, there must be eleven others like him. We chose them as our best. I know! I had a hand in it."

"We had to do it that way, don't you see?" he said. "The party, the whole party, had to believe in it and be convinced that we were getting somewhere near our dream at last. That was what it was for. We needed it, Berkeley. I think you know we did. The party was going down. People can't strive endlessly for an ideal that they can't achieve politically in neither their nor their children's lifetimes."

He was not denying it. He never had. When I had walked in on him, to find him alone in the flat, and had told him I knew about the rocket, he had just accepted it. He who was the most expert and professional liar had not for his own life's sake even attempted a denial.

I felt the bitter dregs of my purpose to kill him grieve like gall.

"Maybe I am too simple to accept this kind of thinking," I said.

He nodded. It was not something to argue about. Some people were like that; they were too simple.

He spoke again in his calm way. While he was turned toward me on the parapet a little light fell on his face from the window of the flat, and I could see he was looking at me oddly. "We are the purveyors of a dream. Have you never understood that?"

There was something incredible to me in his choice of language, and in the way that, in his position, he was admitting things.

"Is that what you call it, our Yellow faith in the perfectibility of man—a dream? Is that how you and the leaders have always regarded it, something to sell and work with, an illusion maybe?"

He was almost gentle. "It isn't a fact, is it? At best it is a hope, about something in the future."

How had we got onto that discussion, to looking at things in that way? I was being given entry to the mind of C. Q. Lankowitz, and I listened almost compulsively, and with a sense of horror.

"There was no dream about the way our people came from Earth to Arcon!" I was bitter. "They believed in the future of man and the universe alike, and they were unlike you. They went ahead and did it!"

"But were they right?" he asked. With a small motion of one shoulder he indicated the Arcon night around us and the city that lay behind him.

It was true that, apart from the emergence of different kinds of minds, minds like that of Len Thomas and C. Q. Lankowitz, I could see no advantage in man's journey from Earth to Arcon.

"We cheated, didn't we, Berkeley?" he said. "We, the Yellow leaders, even when we left Earth? We told our people that men would have to evolve and grow better in a new environment. In fact, we are only becoming different. That is all that happens in new environments to living creatures. Only once in a thousand or a million times does a strain arise with advantages that are general. But we never made much of that point, did we? We let the people understand that their descendants would be better if they made one star-journey once."

How could I express the bitterness with which I heard him?

"Lankowitz, I know why you are saying this. It won't work! You know I am going to kill you, and do you imagine you can destroy me utterly before you go?"

The light reflected for a moment in the shadows of his eyes.

"You are sure you won't destroy yourself after I am gone, Berkeley? If you think that is my aim, you only have to press the trigger to kill me before you hear it."

I knew he was right. I had to kill him then to stop the process of my own disillusion. But that was it. He knew me.

Can any man such as myself, who truly believes he knows and seeks to find the truth, refuse to hear it? He watched me sit there and knew he had me.

"Berkeley," he said, "think."

He knew that what I wished above anything was to stop doing that.

"To make sure that man would really win, and improve, and gain the universe, what would we have had to do?" he asked me. "I will tell you. We would have had to cast ourselves away on the planets of the stars in such numbers, and with such abandon, as our ancestors the fish were driven by predators onto countless shores, to gasp and flap. Nature is incredibly wasteful. You yourself have known that, but have you ever faced it? Think of those fish, our ancestors, the few of the millions coming ashore into shallow seas and onto mud-flats that did not die. What happened to them? They did not evolve into man directly, but into countless species of reptiles, birds and mammals. Yet again, out of all those infinite varieties, only one strain, man, is the one we now regard as having a chance to be successful. What we did was take a chance in a million, Berkeley. And that is the nearest thing to feeding on men's dreams, and selling them a gross illusion."

He was destroying my illusions, and he knew it.

Even before I had come into the Information Office, or learned that the Yellows were still a power on Arcon and that I was not alone, I was a man who had come to Yellow conclusions about my view of the universe and life in general. The Information Office had sought me out, and taken me into itself after I had thought for myself about the development of the stars and the emergence of life and what it all meant. I had known in my heart before men like Lankowitz got me that man had to go on someday, and up, to the farthest stars.

Like Len and his companions, I thought bitterly, who must also have been ready to come to the romantic conclusions inherent in our life on Arcon and our age and time. It was a dream maybe, but if so it was a great dream, in my mind and many others, and I had always envisaged the people of Arcon, even if they did not know it, as living for it, despite themselves, and it was that which Lankowitz was destroying, somewhere deep inside me.

XLIII

ENCLOSED IN THE CAPSULE in the nose cone of the rocket, Len thought that it would be better if they could see out. But they went to their blast-off couches.

They could not see out. It had been explained to them in the space school. It would be more comfortable for them, no doubt, to be able to see out across the desert before the blast-off, to see the hills and the last of Arcon's endless lonely blue horizons, but a space capsule, the space capsule they were using, was a delicate precision instrument. They had a long time ahead in space to think of, and the control dome was almost all glass. It would not do to subject that to abrasion or heat, to say nothing of the chance of anything hitting it, until they were in the emptiness of space itself. That was why they had to start off on the space-shot blind.

Len was not much concerned with the explanation. He merely made sure that Lucinda's blast-off couch was ready, and that Lucinda was near it, and then went up the spiral stair to the control dome, illuminated artificially until the protective sheath came off, where Duncan as pilot, (whose pilot's controls would not operate until they got halfway to Vista and a relay closed), and Salford and Susan and himself, made up the control-deck crew.

Lying down and fastening the straps, he looked at the clock that was one of the instruments in the dome above them, and at the others. Duncan had only been included in the flight because he was the one who, when they came to Vista, would have to make a landing. Salford was there as emergency second pilot because whatever else Salford was, he had the fastest reaction times. Susan was there as mathematical navigator, to operate the flight-deck's small computer. "We are early strapping in," Susan said, also looking at the clock, which showed five minutes to go to blast-off.

The four of them knew one another too well to have much to say in that five minutes. They thought more of the crew scattered at stations throughout the ship. Len checked the navigational instruments and spoke into the phone at one-minute intervals.

"One minute to go." He adjusted the microphone to his mouth and the earpiece to his ear, and lay back at that point. Through the ship, voices, including Lucinda's, were telling him they were set at their blast-off stations.

There was nothing anyone could do about it if they weren't. It had been very thoroughly explained to them that they were not in a position to delay the blast-off.

"Start the one-second countdown, Len," Duncan said.

"If you can slip in a word to David, tell him it was nice to know him," said Susan in a small voice.

"Fifteen, fourteen, thirteen, twelve," Len said.

Blast-off came half a second late by the clock in the control dome.

There was no physical sensation to begin with, except

the noise, which reached them by some route before the heavier vibration that followed it. That was when they missed being able to see out most, when the rocket scream started, and everything around them began to rock with thunder. There was no physical feeling of blast-off until the rocket had burned sufficient of its enormous load of fuel for the thrust to begin to be felt in terms of increasing acceleration.

The vibration was very bad. *We will blow up,* Len thought. He noticed he was thinking, in a kind of angry, despairing way. *If we don't blow up,* he thought distinctly, *then we will shake ourselves to pieces.* He thought of Lucinda, down in her lonely cabin berth. Down there, she was supposed to keep her eye on crew's morale at all times, but just then no one could keep an eye on anything.

Acceleration became worse, in a sequence they had been trained for at the space school. Before black-out it was almost impossible not to give way to panic as a giant hand pressed downward. He fixed his gaze on the clock as long as he could. It was vibrating too, and he wondered if it would come out of its socket, just before he went into black-out.

Coming out again, his sensation was a tumbling fall. The sensation of falling was another cause for panic.

A bang. His mind, which was trying to work again, told him that that was the first stage departing. His feelings, which had been operating first, told him a different story. He guessed that when you came alive to a sensation of free-fall, and there was a bang, the nervous system transmitted the message that you had hit something.

Noise again and harder, faster vibration. That would be the second stage firing, with a smaller load. Where were they now? One thing he was sure of, and that was that they were rapidly heading for black-out a second time.

Somewhere in the upper atmosphere.

Presumably.

Was it not time the cover came off the dome? There was the sensation of free-fall again now. Over the phone, quite distinctly, came Penny's voice. "My light's gone out."

That was because they were existing in a creaking, pinging silence. To Len, it sounded as though the ship were breaking up. Then he realized that, with all the phone microphones that were connected to his ear, he was picking up every creak and ping throughout the ship. It was as well, for one of the two lights in their dome had gone out as well, and he personally felt a sudden lack of confidence in the Arcon engineers.

"We are in space," he announced.

"How do you know?" Salford said in a low voice beside him. It was almost dark.

"Because we are still alive," Susan said, "by logic."

There was a phut or thud, and a tearing sound, and the cover came off the dome and proved it. Relief was blinding.

All around them, through the facets of the glass, they saw the stars. Len stared at it, unbelieving.

"In glorious color," said Salford dryly. His voice was awed.

It was true. Somehow, Len had thought that space would be black and white, white points of stars against a black background. Instead, as well as the colors of the stars, there were wisps and banks of ultraviolet. A gas-cloud, faint and far away, threaded through the star bank, half concealing some stars and revealing others, which gave the scene perspective.

Us, we, in space?

Len had a moment of wonder. Where was Arcon? Away beneath them. And the suns were to the left, below, so that sun-rays cut the dome. Actuality.

"Announce we made it." Duncan's voice was triumphant.

Triumph too soon? Why the awe and thought of warning? Len announced, just factually, "Your captain says we made it."

"Len." It was Lucinda's voice.

Why was it there, in a tone of voice, the something that was expected?

Because space, the starry scene that surrounded the dome, was perfect? What Arcon did was never perfect.

"What is it, dear?"

"Almost everyone's lights are out. Things are not too good down here." There were things unsaid in that tone.

Trouble. The blast-off vibration had been too much. It reflected on the standards to which someone had built the rocket.

"Duncan." Len switched off his microphone and used a low tone. "The crew's lights are out and there are other troubles. Lucinda is doubtful of things below decks."

Duncan, sitting up on his blast-off couch, was releasing his straps and looking out at the starry heavens. They were there, weren't they? In space. He looked at Len, looking for what was unsaid in Len's voice.

They had begun to feel a light, very light, thrust of acceleration gravity, which should go on increasing.

Sorensen, in Len's ear, reported that the atomic motors had started. Doubtfully, he mentioned the machine-deck instruments. They should feel the major thrust of the ion-beam.

Duncan looked at his instruments silently. They were now under ground control from the radio telescope, and their sensation of personal weight should rise soon, as acceleration increased, to something like three-fifths of normal gravity. It did not happen.

Instead of telling Sorensen or Ropotsky to break out the electrical spares and repair the lights. Duncan said, "Tell the machine-deck crew to examine everything they can to see how it is functioning, then to come up here and report to me. Tell the girls, if they can find their way, to come up here for a little while." It was an order.

Susan was asking Len to use his navigational instruments to take sights on Arcon, Arcon's suns, and fixed stars, so that she could compute their velocity and course at take-off. Len relayed Duncan's message first. The pilots had retro-mirrors that came into action now that the casing was off the space vehicle, and by using them, as would in theory when making a landing on a planet, they could obtain a full view of Arcon. Salford had suddenly gone silent and was staring with great concentration at the view behind them.

While Len began to take the navigational sights for Susan, who fed them into her computer, the crew from below decks began to come up. No one in the control dome had had time to try any walking yet. Len only realized how difficult it was when he saw Lucinda, balancing like a high-wire artist, coming across to his couch. Accelerating away toward the speed of light, a process that would take weeks, it should have been almost normal.

No one knew whether it was a good thing or a bad that almost all the crew was on the control deck when they discovered the truth about things. They would have had to be told anyway.

Sorensen had come up and was standing by Duncan's couch, reporting to him and holding onto it to keep his balance.

"All the machine-deck instruments are reporting full power from the atomic motors. It looks as though this is all the thrust we are going to get."

Salford said, "Len, will any of your instruments look

backward, and give you a close view of the detail of our own ship's tail?"

It was not warning in Salford's voice. It was something not heard before from Salford.

Len and Lucinda looked at one another. Fear?

Take it easy, Len thought. Lucinda, who had come to stand by his couch, thought it better to hold on to it. They exchanged a glance again, and she looked at Salford. Her eyes asked, "Is he one of us?" It would be a bad time to find out that the twenty-four-legged monster, might or might not exist in Lucinda's mind, was lame in two of its legs.

Len moved the instruments that glittered above him in the stark light of the starlit dome. There was something unhomely in everything that was happening now. "The short-range rangefinder landing periscope should do it, Des."

He looked through the eyepiece. The first thing he saw was Arcon, with their ion-beam train trailing away toward it. It was a slender, almost invisible trail for their rocket there in space to stand on. As he adjusted the instrument the tail of their own ship came into view, and the long thin hull containing the atomic motors. He saw what Salford meant then, but Salford did not give him time to remark on it.

They wouldn't do that to us, Len thought.

"We are in space all right," Salford said. If there was anyone who had not been paying attention, they would be then.

"But this ship isn't built right. Maybe someone wanted to economize. Or maybe they couldn't get enough lift from the blast-off rockets. We are missing some items, such as the landing rocket stages we would need to land on any planet—which means we are in space forever."

It was natural that Salford should be sounding as though he did not like it.

"It seems to be very final. There isn't a spaceship even to rescue us, is there?" Lucinda said in a mild, disbelieving way that asked them to be calm about it.

Len gulped a little.

"We are lost in space," Salford said with drama. "We are in a worse spot than anyone has been in, and it's impossible to get us out of it. What use are your electric bits and pieces now, Len, when we have no means for landing?"

Looking out into space, Len could see that it no longer
129

mattered who controlled the rocket, which he had intended to do, when they could not land it. "Now, Des," he said, "let's think a little."

XLIV

From *The Short History of Arcon*:

Unfortunate and tragic as events were, it is necessary to be objective. It is surely agreed that the minds of men on Earth were barely human, and this fact should be noted when considering the further development that occurred on Arcon. We can hardly deny, when we consider the fated starship crew, a mental change of some kind.

Compare them with Earth mentality, for example. It is the slowness, the lack of grasp of a situation, which seems impossible to us, in what we know of Earth. The men of Earth found it impossible to grasp even major facts. Aggression continued on Earth long after the biological need for it had been expended, and when sheer human survival alone demanded that mutual competition should cease, and that men should work together for mere existence. Yet men on Earth seem to have given no thought at all to the fact that they were no longer striving to become, but had long ago achieved the position of a dominant species. Men said it, but failed utterly to realize the implications.

Contrast this with the behavior of the young people in the spacecraft known as Arcon One. The point is the speed with which they began to think of their own situation in planetary, stellar, and cosmic terms. It is not merely a matter of higher mental freedom, but of a wider frame of reference. They were still men and women. They were inexperienced men and women. It might even be true to say that they were innocent men and women. Yet, in their viewing of their own situation, there was a certain freedom that was not merely freedom, but a building-up of structure. Lacking a mental framework into which to place their problems, they rapidly built one. And there was nothing artificial about this. The behavior-pattern was not laborious or mechanistic. Apart from the deviation of the one of their number who was a substitute, it was completely *natural*.

And ship-shape, as we would now say, in Vista fashion.

XLV

From the diary of J. Adolf Koln:

September 6, 506 A. L. Noon.
The waiting is over, finally. At the moment of blast-off, even now as I sit at this desk in my office in the Hexagon and look out on Davis City, the parachute troops who have ringed all the radio telescopes, and especially the one at the rocket project, will be closing in on them, arriving in their positions, and preparing for a coup that will be as effective as it will be almost bloodless.

The steps of the operation are clear, and have been checked and double-checked. First they, the Information Office, must get the rocket in space, and have control of it. In this operation, Glasson must play his vital role. He must see that the Information Office technicians are present in the telecommunications building, and working, at the time our men cut the telephones and stop their communications. Nothing must be done until the rocket is in space, and he is to see that with his own eyes, then send the signal "Go" to us.

2 P.M.
The signal has come! I have just received it by the telephone on my desk. The rocket has gone up, and the signal was "Successful," which means Glasson has assured himself that not merely has it left the atmosphere and attained escape velocity, but the radio telescope has control of it. All I want now are the confirming signals from the Second Army and the Swamp Corps.

Glasson must not move until tonight. As soon as the I. O. phones are cut, we can imagine that there will be protest and disturbance. They cannot possibly guess what we intend to do, but they will know that we intend something. That is why the takeover of the telecommunications and the radio telescopes must follow swiftly on the cutting of the land-lines and progress completely smoothly. The technicians who are trained to operate the equipment must be taken alive, to continue to work it, with a gun at their backs and one of our own experts standing over each of them. I have gone into this in detail with Pintopler, 38239 - Z, who is our double-agent.

Nothing can stop me now except a defect, a mis-

calculation that would be purely technical. If I have fears, they are only that the planet's fate could possibly be decided by some outside chance. Yet our calculations are exact. It is only a matter of deciding how far the rocket must go, between blast-off, which was three hours ago, and the time we turn it over and start to bring it back to land on Arcon. Surely no chance can enter when all of this is mathematical science and we know the answers.

Pintopler is the one who, acting for us, has worked it out in detail. The rocket will have to lose the velocity it has acquired. First it must be made to slow down. Then it will start to fall back onto the planet, with an increasing acceleration that, if we did not check it with the retrorockets of the stage used for landing, would rapidly take it to too high a speed. It is not that I know about the retrorockets and landing stages, but Pintopler assures me that they are all there in the radio telescope controls, and marked with their dials and switches, which is as well. Without them, the rocket would continue to fall, and burn like a meteor, and explode on landing. A massive deceleration is required at that point, so that we can bring the capsule down slowly, and land it precisely in Davis City, as a spectacle. I do not see what can interfere with this, and it is fortunate that the space crew cannot, for if they did they would be dead on their arrival.

XLVI

From *The Jottings of G. Berkeley:*

Lankowitz knew me. I could see that by the way he sat on the parapet and continued the process of my disillusion. Maybe he was taking a calculated risk. He could not know me with complete certainty, and another man, facing the loss of his faith, would certainly have lifted his gun and shot him.

It was a question of what was my faith, and what part truth played in it. He could only guess, not know, that I had a compulsion to discover truth. Not many men have. The majority would rather kill any day than have their faith destroyed, and the fact that they know in their minds that it is the truth they are being told does not decrease the impulse.

"Face it, Berkeley," he said in his careful way. "You

know, really, what our predecessors did, when they led men from Earth to Arcon. They sold them a dream, man's own dream, which he wished to believe in. They lied to them, and they were able to do it because men wished to believe the lies they told them."

For moments, when he was talking, I saw his dark figure as a spider, spinning its own web as they say an Earth spider does, out of its own substance, to enmesh and seal the fate of innocents. Those were the times I wished to kill him.

"That is what all exponents of political and religious faiths have done," he told me. "Cut the logical and factual corners, and emphasized the half-truths. The skill is to make the dream look real, and use emotion and the natural human longing for some half-glimpsed ideal to cover up the blind spots."

Yet I could not kill him until he had said it, until I had given him a chance to say it.

"How true were the dreams men have sold in the past?" he asked me. "Life after death, and the reassembly of those particular molecules that compose our bodies? Would you have said Earth's dream of communism would have worked, with every man contributing willingly to every other man's needs, except by a change in the human spirit? And was it truly possible to change that spirit by the system of preaching love, the alternative, against the dogma background of a next world, resurrection, and rewards in heaven? These dreams were no more true, and just a shade more wild than ours, yet they engaged the minds and hearts of men for centuries, for all that they moved them forward."

I could see him looking at me almost wistfully in the half-light, as though I were one of the few, and one whom he had selected, perhaps, to understand him. He spoke as though he had been intending for a long time to have this talk with me. He gestured as though to say, "Be practical."

"We led men from Earth, Berkeley," he told me calmly, "as I am told someone called Moses once led a people into a desert. It may even have been a surprise to Moses that they acted on his dreams and followed blindly. And when that happens, the leaders are stuck with it, and must live with it, and face the people's disillusion. Sustaining a religion then is not a matter of preaching. It becomes a desperate business, and a matter of compromising with the state, the power. Think what happened to us on Arcon, while we ourselves were facing the fact that to make our dream come true we might have to send a million expeditions to a million stars, so that one might be successful. This was the time we became a decaying, defeated, reviled and persecuted party."

Looking at him, and comparing him with what I believed I knew, I said, "But that was the time of your ancestor, your noble ancestor, the other Lankowitz," and he heard my pride.

He looked at me quietly for a moment. "So you know that piece of history."

He was looking at me as though I was the kind of man who would know.

"I will tell you the truth. Do you think he was a saint, this Lankowitz who revived our party? He lived at a time when a man had only to express a Yellow opinion to be tarred and feathered, and he had trouble with his own beliefs. But he was a salesman, with business acumen. He invented a saying which we have in our family. 'In time of doubt and despair,' he used to say, 'that is the time a good man will go out and cross his heart and tell an untruth boldly.'"

I could see his dark eyes watching me as though he saw my idols falling.

"You mean that he had only that kind of courage to face the lynch-mobs?"

"He never faced the lynch-mobs. He was the kind of second-man who comes in every political party or great religion. The man who uses, and makes a business, of a faith that was sincerely meant before him. You know what he did. He took us over to the government side. He took us into the Information Office, where the politicians in the know tolerate us. And do you know why they tolerate us? Because we are like the priesthood of an established church. They see us as like those Christians, preaching love and forgiveness of enemies, who used to bless the battleships and bombers, and crown the monarchs, and confirm their power. We are like the social-democrats, who paid lip-service to a revolutionary creed, but helped to maintain the established order. He gave us a function in the Arcon state. To identify, enroll, emasculate and, so they believe, mislead the active Yellows."

What I could not see was how he could sit there and speak in those terms of the ruin of a once-mighty party that had at one time moved men across the cosmos.

"You are telling me that you, the pope of our religion, are an atheist, and therefore I should kill you."

He did not hurry to answer me. He seemed to contemplate it, as though it might be true.

"What I am saying is that they have only a limited validity, conditional and restricted and outworn, the things that you believed in. We Yellows are like those ancient priests who also sold better lives in another world. And it is only if you see this that you can start again at the beginning."

I stared at the city, the lights in the darkness beyond the wall, in which I had lived and which I had thought I had understood. "Beginning? Just what beginning?"

He had to talk quickly then, before I pressed the trigger, but he did not seem to hurry.

"I told you that some man must stand up, and cross his heart, and tell an untruth boldly. It is what the leaders of the old religions did. They promised an afterlife, and do you think they were wrong to say that dream was possible? 'Be good,' you remember they told their people, 'and believe in miracles.' Be merciful, and yield to justice, truth and beauty, and you will find your reward in heaven. It was a lie, and do you think they didn't know it, at least fifty percent of the time, at the time they said it?" His voice slowed down; he risked it. "But see what happened." He told me then.

"Sometimes, not always but sometimes, some justice or goodness or truth resulted. And this was on the savage planet Earth, remember. This was in a land where animal instincts were still unbridled, and where 'natural' life was ruthlessness, cruelty, and pure rapine. It was not those who had the truth that had the courage, you see, it was the liars. Whatever shifts they were forced to, to tell their lies, and whatever imagination they had to use to tell them. Because out of nothing came something. The beauty was not there, and then it was there. They inspired belief in the impossible, and then they got it, a very little." I was startled to see tears in his eyes.

It was true I had not dreamed of such an excuse before.

I had not previously heard the virtue of the lie expounded, on the grounds that it could be creative.

I wondered what kind of world he inhabited, and what kind of man he was, this person I saw in silhouette against the city lights. What cosmos was it, where the will entered deliberately into his objective view, and shaped the mental constructions that he carved in that darkness he called reality?

"You must understand these things." He was persuasive.

"It's not only because you may kill me that I am telling you the truth. It's more that I don't want not to leave anything behind me. I would have had to tell you all this sooner or later, since I see you as my successor."

I could only believe he was lying. It was far too cheap and easy. I found it quite incredible.

"You think that is how to talk me out of your execution?" We were back from the depths of time again.

He laughed in my face. "We have often killed one another at the head of the Yellow Party." Then he was serious. "Remember the General. I tell you again, he is not the man to try to use us for a little thing. Think, Berkeley. Think. Why did he offer a rocket project to the Yellow Party?" He watched me as he told me. "It could only be to expose us. And that in some dramatic way. To wait till we sent a rocket up, and then bring it down again maybe? It would be so easy for him to take over from us in the desert project. This is only a guess. If you ask me if I've proof, I haven't. I have only the fact that if the rocket was produced, with an Arcon crew chosen by the Information Office getting out of it, it would be enough to cause the government to fall.

He was watching me with narrowed eyes and extremely closely. By then, he knew he had me.

"What was needed from the party point of view, Berkeley? A successful space-shot? One that would go away and land on a distant planet somewhere? Not all of that was necessary to serve the dream. The time of interstellar voyages is such that it was only necessary that it should go up, and not be heard of. It was gratuitous, it was also safer, when circumstances forced us that way, that it would have to be a rocket that would not fly anywhere and that could not be landed. It was not that we could do the other thing. We only did what we could to save the dream, the party."

XLVII

What do we do now, after Salford has pointed out that it is impossible for anyone to land us, Len thought? Maybe a beast was dancing.

It was not a good analogy, but it was the best he could think of in space, looking at Lucinda as she stood by his couch, with a surround of black sky and stars around her. Irrelevantly he thought, *There are too many stars.*

In fact, the conversation that was taking place was impossible. The way it seemed to him, it was impossible that they should hold a conversation at all after Salford had pointed out their situation. Penny and Susan, Duncan, Ropotsky, Harold Sorensen and all the rest were looking thoughtful. What they ought to be doing, he could not help feeling, was throwing fits of hysteria. Maybe it was because they kept their mouths shut that Salford was the only one so far to show himself as heated, and that did not make sense. Len had a vision of the twenty-four-legged beast, last seen sniffing the flowers, now taking a look at the universe from the better vantage point of space itself. *Or am I mad?* Len thought. *I must be.*

"You don't understand," Salford said, staring at them. "We are stuck in space, and it's impossible we should land anywhere except as a crash or a streak of fire."

Ropotsky looked solemn. It was an important subject. To them it was very important. They did not want to rush it.

Mad, Len thought, looking at the people in the control dome. *Not only me, all of them.* Or would they improve things by screaming?

"It's what people said about going to the moon, once," Sorensen said helpfully to Ropotsky.

Imantha looked strained. "Des just said it's impossible for anyone to rescue us," she said.

In the control dome of the spaceship, lost in space, not getting anywhere, and with no means to land, no one seemed to think that Salford had much reason for the excuse that Imantha made for him.

"Like someone has to say 'impossible,' so they can take a look at the problem, and see what it is, and start to solve it," Ropotsky said to Sorensen.

Len thought: *Not Lucinda.*

She was going to say something. He could see the signs. And he had always thought her a sensible person.

"You are right there, David. That's how it works," she said most carefully.

Maybe he had better look out of the glass of the dome at the star field, and think how infinite it was, Len thought. They would have him doing it next.

"Listen," said Salford. "Or aren't you listening? I'm talking sense."

"Now, Des," said Duncan. "Don't interrupt people, when you can see that they are thinking."

The stars did not seem to change much as Len looked out into space at them. It was true what people said about them, Len thought as he made room for Lucinda on his couch, that they were eternal.

Collectively, that was. Not individually.

"How do you propose to get down onto a planet?" Salford said to Duncan. "Any planet, anywhere?" He too seemed affected. He was not talking violently anymore. He just wanted to know, anxiously.

Don't answer that, Len thought. *He got the idea. Don't jump the gun. There was plenty of time for it.*

In fact, not to put too fine a point on it, eternity.

"Not just any planet," he said to Salford. "A Vista planet. That's where we were going, isn't it?"

Salford looked as though he had thought perhaps everyone else was mad, but not Len, and now Len was too.

" 'Impossible,' " Ed Creet said thoughtfully, as though trying out the word.

Lucinda looked at Len for a while. Then she sat down on the space on the couch that Len had made for her. Duncan seemed to think he was missing something, and draped his arm around Penny's shoulder. Susan, with Ropotsky sitting beside her, put a sum through the ship's computer.

"To get to Vista at our present rate of progress," Susan said, "would take us two hundred and fifty-nine years, nine months." She looked critically at the punched tape the computer produced. "That is, excluding the landing we haven't the means for."

Ropotsky seemed to regard that as a helpful addition to the discussion, but perhaps he was prejudiced in Susan's favor. No one else did.

Len wondered what Lucinda was doing. She was going to talk again, and he hoped it would be a little better.

" 'Impossible' comes from the old style of human thinking," Lucinda said to Ed Creet.

Ed looked interested.

"Traditional," Lucinda explained. "They had several ways of thinking about things, you know, seven or eight. When they had run over them, and none of them worked, they used that word, 'impossible.' "

"I see," Ed said.

"Naturally, we wouldn't do that," Lucinda said.

Len did not know what everyone else was doing. He was sitting and looking at Lucinda, wondering what was inside her, and trying to decide, since it seemed an interesting question, what they would do.

"Different?" Ed said.

Lucinda shook her head over it. Apparently it was different. The spaceship, in Len's estimation, covered another hundred miles or two.

He looked out at the stars and tried to pick out Arcon's fellow planets and decide how long it would take them to get out of Arcon's solar system. Duncan was looking around at the company of his crew as though he thought it was high time someone said something helpful.

It was true that they wanted to go carefully, but not so carefully as to stop altogether in a paralysis of space-fright.

"Suppose you explain to us, Lucinda," Ed Creet said, "what other way we might think, I mean, supposing we aren't going to think in the old way, that used to include 'impossible.' "

Maybe Lucinda knew about it in her psycho-social training, Len thought. He was damned if he did.

"You see, if you say 'impossible,' it means you have preconceptions," Lucinda said. "You lack faith, for one thing, and for another you are probably thinking in terms of superstitions. All history shows that. People were thinking in terms of superstitions or preconceptions when they said man couldn't fly, or go to the moon or stars or such things."

A psychoanalysis of linguistics, Len thought. He looked at the stars. Well, they had time for it. If they didn't do it, they weren't going to get anywhere any sooner.

"So you don't have preconceptions?" Eliza Teen said hopefully.

"You can't help but have them," Lucinda said. To Len's eyes she looked thoughtful, as though trying to recall her training. "I think I know what you do about them. You examine them."

"Personally, I have a lot of preconceptions," Salford said. "That would take a little time."

Who asked Salford to speak? They knew what to do: ignore him.

"Even so, it is rather a tall order," Ropotsky said.

"We might try concentrating on the useful ones," Sorensen said.

"I am not sure there are any useful preconceptions," Lucinda said. "I forget the rule about that."

Shame, Len thought, looking at his girl in the doomed star-dome. *A broken reed.*

"The productive ones, then," Sorensen said.

Salford looked at them and space and said, "What are our preconceptions, anyway, useful or otherwise?" Len

at him with surprise. If Salford was not careful, he
going to start making remarks that were almost useful.
That this spaceship is doomed," Imantha said.

Lucinda's profile looked troubled as Len watched it a-
gainst the stars. "I don't know," she said. "I can't help
feeling. I don't see how we can get out of that."

Or out of the spaceship either, Len thought, looking at
the dark, invisible vacuum of space beyond the glass dome.
Their captors would hardly have sent them up in the rocket
if they were going to provide them with air-supply space-
suits with helmets.

"Maybe we had better look at some other preconceptions," he suggested.

"Such as we can't get another spaceship," Penny remarked innocently.

Len looked thoughtfully at innocent little Penny.

"Only Arcon could supply that," Ropotsky said. "And
Arcon won't."

"That's a preconception," Len said.

"Hell," Ed Creet said. "You'd have to change Arcon to
get them to send us another spaceship."

It was not only Len. They all looked at Ed Creet then.

For some reason Len felt under his couch, where he
had put his small transistors and the other items they had
smuggled aboard the starship.

XLVIII

From *The Short History of Arcon*:

As well as the difference in mental attitudes, there is
also the problem of what can be called the logic of physical circumstances. This is a thread running through the
whole of human history which runs back into the nonorgan-
ic world and also stretches tenuously into the future. To
pursue this line of reasoning, the physical, chemical and
mechanical events are described as a chain of causation,
while the human personalities involved are treated as though
each were a true computer.

It is remarkable, when events are seen in this light, how
circumstances seem to conspire, not in any random way,
but positively to create the next stage of history. It is granted
that there is an illusion about this. We deceive ourselves
if we say how remarkable it was that when the universe
consisted of a tenuous cloud of gas, and a very specific
and mathematically exact force of gravity was required

to make the stars, then it so happened that just that specific force of gravity was there, and no other cause or logic. The obvious answer is that had some other force been in operation, then some different universe would have been created. But the causation chains involved do sometimes seem to have been very long and strange.

Man could not have evolved on Earth, for example, except that the planet was stabilized, over an extremely long period, within a very narrow band of temperatures. The possible temperatures range from absolute zero to figures in the hundred thousands, yet for about a thousand million years Earth had to stay within the few degrees between the freezing point of water and less than halfway to its point of boiling. The atmosphere had first to be a methane mixture for life to start at all, and then to change itself to oxygen as plants developed. The solar radiation reaching the surface had first to be high, to start the molecular reactions, and then to decrease, so that the newly formed compounds could stabilize into living things. A layer of ozone had to appear in the upper atmosphere to reduce the radiation so that mutation would not occur too rapidly and species could develop. The hothouse climate of the carboniferous age had to persist for a long period or the development of reptile life would have been impossible, yet when reptiles had developed to a certain point, the climate had to change so that an advantage could be given to the internal temperature-control system of the evolving mammals.

The solar radiation reaching the Earth had to fluctuate so that periods of rapid evolution, when new species were formed, could be succeeded by "quiet" ages when life forms could consolidate and engage in competition. At no time could the radiation rise that very small percentage which would have destroyed surface life altogether. Man had to be born into a wooded world so as to acquire his opposable thumb and fingers, and then a change had to take place to drive him from the trees so that he could acquire his upright posture. The ice ages were necessary, and just at the right time, so that he should be forced to use tools and fire, and make clothes of the skins of his prey for sheer survival. Too early, and he would not have been sufficiently developed to survive as a tool-making creature; too late, and he would have become too specialized in a fixed way of life and been incapable of the right adaptation. He had to conquer Earth completely in order ever to find himself in the position of being able to leave it for the stars, yet his history had to be such that he was dissatisfied with peace and plenty when he got it: too much aggression, and man would have wiped himself out; too little and he would never have left his own solar system.

In view of circumstances like these, we should not be surprised that the planet man descended on was Arcon, where he found himself faced with a mental challenge of precisely the right kind to force him to take charge of his own destiny in the future. It was one coincidence added to so many other coincidences that it all but makes us believe in predestiny. But we must face the fact that so numerous are the stars in a galaxy, and so infinite the number of galaxies, that had these things not happened to man, they would certainly, in an infinity of time, have happened to some other creature, somewhere else.

XLIX

From the diary:

September 7, 506 A. L.

Dawn.

"The reports are coming in, General. The desert group has changed its position in the night and is moving toward the city. The Swamp Corps is lying beyond the islands. Around the park, the military police have been posted inconspicuously, prepared to control the traffic."

This is it, the day of destiny, the day of triumph.

From my bed in the Hexagon, I rise and go to the window to look out to the southward, across the rooftops and toward the swamplands. There is a haze in the morning light, not mist but soft and luminous. I have the window opened, so I can smell the morning smells. Is there blood in the air? The city still sleeps, unknowing. The aroma is that of our Arcon dust, and men.

"What of Glasson? You have a report from the colonel?"

"Yes, sir. It reads, 'The building below the bowl has been taken and we hold the hill.'"

We have it! We are committed! My mind moves quickly.

It is there, in the desert, that the operation's heart is beating, while I, looking out across the city here to pick out the Senate's dome, am just the brain.

I remember the walls of that space school building when last I saw it, and the skeleton of the rocket gantry

142

that was rising at that time in the desert valley. Men moving on those barren hills on the rock and in the Arcon sand, good men, not knowing what they did or why they did it, except that they had my orders.

Did they wonder last night, when the shadows stretched out across the valley, and they were told to spend the night in the open, with the rocket gone?

"Alert." The word must have been passed down the ranks. As though I were there, I know it. "No lights, no movement until one A.M. You will be required to attack at that time." I wish I had been there, in the desert night, to hear or give those orders.

Attack.

The silent movement of men in darkness. The cutting of the telephone wires. The occupation and blocking of all the desert tracks that out there they call the roads. The occupation of the Information Office, the space school, and then suddenly the entry of armed men into the building on the hill, coming out of the night, from nowhere.

The radio telescope bowls still pointing at the sky and holding on the rocket, but under new orders now.

The Information Office must know of it, but what can they do? "Communication has gone dead to the space project and the radio telescopes, sir." But it will not be a very important man who is on duty there at this hour. "Try to establish communication by other routes." He will be sleepy and unwilling to take responsibility. "See to it that the engineers are warned, but tell them not to dispatch anyone until they get their orders from the day-shift."

These people, waking and rising in the city, do not know what day this is.

The rocket should be turning over in the sky now. I visualize it, checking its momentum and preparing to swoop down on Arcon, much quicker to fall than it was to go up and leave us. And the city waits, unknowing.

L

The Jottings:

"Come," he said, looking to where the dawn was rising. "You and I must go back to the office. We must control the situation. Even though the General does not get the rocket, he may still make some move."

It was true that, seen from the rooftop, the city lights were paler. When I turned my head, I could see the light in the eastern sky.

"You expect me to put my gun away and trust you?"

"Come, Berkeley. Even you must see that your life is of little account in all this."

I still thought he might find time to touch a button and call his guard and have me arrested.

I put my gun away and got up and walked away from him, to the eastern parapet where I could watch the dawn arising along the swamp shore. I did not look at what he was doing. He would be armed, I thought, and I might fall forward. He came to stand beside me.

So he had not killed me.

"This night's events have confirmed my view that you will be my successor, Berkeley. You will be surprised to hear how few men I know who are prepared to put anything above their own lives, or, something I have never been able to understand, above the lives of other people."

I wondered.

I wondered if it would not have been better if I had killed him or he had killed me when we had the chance.

"It is not whether we kill or let innocents suffer," he said while we looked out over the still dark swamp-groves to the dawning sky. "The question for our kind is whether we wish to wrap some illusory sanctity around ourselves, and pretend we would not hurt a fly, while we let the generals kill them."

LI

IN THE SPACE DOME, Salford looked at the company, got up and walked to the edge of the deck, from where, standing against the dome, he could look out and downward at Arcon's blazing suns. He could not see Arcon down there, for Arcon was so far beneath them as to be seen only in the retro-mirrors, but for a moment, as he looked around again at the star field, they must have seemed to be lost in a sky of blackness.

"What are you talking about, 'alternating Arcon'?" he asked them. "Changing a world?" For once, Salford looked at them as though making an appeal to reason. "Wouldn't we all have liked to do it while we were in Arcon, change the world around us? And now we are not even on it."

Len looked in the retro-mirror and saw the blue iridescent disk of Arcon that swam in the bowl of stars below them.

144

That was how their ancestors must have seen it, he thought, at the time of landing.

"I agree," he said deliberately. "It's a tall order at any time, to change a world."

But, unlike Salford, he did not say it was impossible. And Salford did not look at him as though what he said was an agreement.

"We have left it. We aren't on it, and now we can't affect it." Salford waved a hand at the space that they inhabited. "We can't affect it in any way!"

There was a silence as there always was when Salford raised his voice a little.

Eliza Teen moved and sat forward from the edge of the deck where she had been resting her back against the rim of the metal wall that supported the dome above them. She sounded thoughtful.

"Besides, if they did build another ship, if we so changed them that they built another ship for us, it would take them years. How many years would we have to wait for it?"

There was that too, but Duncan did not like it. He looked obstinate, as though he did not like anyone carping at any positive suggestion. "If the way to deal with things is to alter Arcon, then we must alter Arcon."

"How?" said Salford.

No one expected little Penny to tell them. Penny was the kind of girl who had one idea in her life, and then it was completely obvious, and she looked at Duncan with big, round eyes.

But Penny was there, with them.

"We could send out an S.O.S.," she said.

LII

The Shopping Lists:

Important.

To Whom It May Concern.

This note will probably be seen first by whoever eventually breaks into this flat. It is a suicide note. It should be reported to the police. Or preferably it should be left where it is, and the police told where to find my body.

145

LIII

The Jottings:

We went to the Information Office building, and through the day of the sixth and the morning of the seventh we tried to deal with contingencies that were imponderable and events we did not know because they had not happened yet.

That was Lankowitz and I working, he with intensity and I unwillingly.

He came into my office in the afternoon of the sixth on his way to the Senate. I noticed then that he was a little disturbed. What he was about to do was visit the leader of the Senate to warn him that the army was likely to revolt the following day. He had to do it with such tact and discretion as not to reveal his lack of evidence for what I still regarded as his guess or gross assumption.

"It has occurred to me, Berkeley, that if the General brings the rocket back, he'll find it impossible to stop it, so it will come down like a fireball and explode on landing."

I looked at him bitterly, knowing the truth of that.

"You can just say that? You're telling me it will be a merciful death for those inside the rocket?"

He looked at me with dry patience, as though I were being awkward too, as well as other people.

"What is important is that the atomic drive units are not detachable from the living quarters. We had to leave that out too. Do you think there will be an atomic fallout?"

I stared at him and the papers on the desk before me.

"Do you know what the army is doing? Look at this. The army has arranged its major show right here, in Central Park in Davis City. Do you know what you are saying?"

His eyes watched me in their narrow way. "You suggest I convey that in a minor aside to the Senate leader?" He turned to the door, thoughtfully looking back at me again.

"You are so concerned with the youngsters in the rocket that you haven't thought of the city and the hundred thousand or two million people, with ourselves among them?"

He went out, leaving me to envisage the explosion of the rocket fireball.

It seemed unreal, a nightmare. The papers before me told of the Army Day celebrations, which always called out a crowd, and which were arranged for a time that it was easy to calculate as the right one, in Central Park. I had to try to believe that I was expected to plan for such contingencies.

As though the human mind could encompass it, in terms of mere statistics. It felt like theory, not actuality. To satisfy him, I thought of what he would do, if he were dealing with the practical Capital District work instead of me. I saw that he would consider security first, and so I gave orders to move our headquarters temporarily to the emergency building we kept for the purpose at the place called Parker's Knoll, outside the city.

I was accepting it and conniving at the death of Len Thomas, on Lankowitz' instructions.

LIV

The diary:

September 7, 506 A. L.

1:55 P.M.
Everything should go perfectly, but does it ever?

2:00 P.M.
From my window I watch the sky. This is the hour the rocket should be landing. The troops are assembled in Central Park. This is it. The military policemen are assembled at the crossroads. The light-armored troops are pouring in from the desert, and working their way into the city.

2:01 P.M.
What anguished fate is this?
Something has gone wrong. I have just had a belated message from Colonel Glasson. The rocket, which had turned over in the sky, in response to signals from the telescope, has suddenly veered off. It seems impossible. Glasson reports his technicians are working on it. He was delayed in calling by having to have a group of I. O. technicians taken out and shot.
First the rocket varied its course. Then it appeared that it was going into an orbit. It is since then that it has changed course again, and now it is heading again for Vista.
I must have Glasson shot. How can the rocket possibly be carrying on to Vista? Only the radio telescope

147

could make it do that. It is impossible to understand the situation in the desert there.

2:05 P.M.

What am I to do now? I have my troops pouring into the city. I have crowds assembled in Central Park on the promise that the Army Spectacular this year will really be a show. Worse than that, two more disturbing reports have just come in to me. Our unit surrounding the Information Office, ready to go in and take over the moment the rocket landed, apparently became suspicious. They sent men in, who have reported that there is only a skeleton staff present and the building is virtually deserted. And the Senate, which had decided to sit at this hour, has apparently suspended its sitting and retired into the basement.

This is the moment of destiny, when a man who is a man must decide either to go back or forward.

There is a tide in the affairs of men. Having assembled my forces for this moment, I know with sudden certainty that I will not have this chance again. For other men at other times a chance will come, but my time is now.

2:10 P.M.

I have done it. I have ordered our men in contact with the broadcasting services to stand by for a grave announcement of planetwide importance, that will be made in five minutes. We have the facilities laid on, and I propose to use them. All channels will carry the statement I will make from this office, through the microphones and cameras trained on my desk here.

I have also caused an announcement to be made in Central Park. Crowds of that kind always have their portable and pocket radios with them, and the request has been made over the public address system that they turn them on. They must feel that they are connected directly to me by personal coverage. This is the crowd I intend to use to march on the Senate building— where their Senators are cowering in the basement! And I will use them. It is up to me now.

LV

*Official Text of the Plain Language
Distress Messages from* Arcon One:

First Message, timed 2:13:
S.O.S. S.O.S. S.O.S. From the Spaceship *Arcon One.* Attacked.

This message was repeated several times on frequencies
audible through popular broadcast stations. From the first,
the transmission had the nature of a public appeal, and
the location of the transmitting station could be established
by tilting a portable radio upward. Later, the indication
was given, "Listen on 1000 kilocycles."

Second Message, timed 2:14:
S. O. S. From the Arcon Spaceship *Arcon One.* Attacked
by three unknown space vessels at distance of five thousand
miles from Arcon. Have received hit and damage to stern.

Third Message, timed 2:30:
S.O.S. S.O.S. S.O.S. From spaceship *Arcon One.* Enemy
vessels are closing with us. Fear this is the end. Warn the
Arcon people of their peril. Goodbye.

Fourth Message, timed 2:45:
Arcon One. Enemy vessels have examined our damage
and departed. We are out of control, under low power,
and drifting away in the direction of the star Vista, toward
which enemy last seen departing. Six girls on board. Vital
that we receive help.

LVI

The star dome was less crowded since Lucinda had established her script-writing team on the cabin-deck; and since
the ground-control signals from the radio telescope had
been jammed by the low-power spark transmitter in Salford's charge, Arcon had appeared like the disk of a rising
moon on the edge of the star field of the dome.

"Go back and tell them this is pure corn," Duncan said,
reading the text of the latest message that the script team
of Lucinda, Vera and Eliza had produced from their artis-

tic workshop on the deck below. He looked at Penny, who had brought the message, as though she were responsible for the production of the literary masterminds. "They aren't even pretending to use international distress procedure any more."

"Lucinda says it has to be corny," Penny said, defending her department. "It's for popular appeal. It's a kind of psycho-social principle."

"Let's only hope they can hear it at all," Susan said, struggling with a technical and mathematical problem Len had set her on a computer that was not designed for it.

Len was on the phone to Sorensen and the engineering team on the machine-deck of the ship. "Another message coming up. Look, give us real power this time. It doesn't matter if you stop the air-pumps and Ropotsky's bio-tank lights and heaters for a little time."

Looking out of the dome at the long wire antennae which now trailed away from the ship, and which sometimes showed a tendency to tangle since they were mostly stripped from the lighting circuits, Imantha performed her technical function by saying, "Now."

"Stand by," said Duncan, and put on the expression he used when he tried to sound like a golden-voiced hero, which was the way Lucinda had depicted the character he had to assume for their transmissions.

The lights went dim inside the ship as Len threw the switch that had once been part of the pilots' control system. Outside the ship, and around the metal hull, a faint blue glow appeared, for Len, faced with the problem of constructing a giant transmitter tube, had decided to use space itself as the vacuum. From below decks, over the phone, came a sound of exclamations, and an electronic hiss and spitting. The insulated plugs through which the electrodes had been pushed outside the hull were not quite as perfect as they might have been.

"Emergency, emergency, emergency," Duncan said, reading the script Penny had given him into the microphone she held before him. "From the captain of Arcon One . . ."

"Increase the modulation," Len said, looking at his instruments and speaking to his electronic team. "It will sound more realistic if there's some distortion."

The operation for changing Arcon, based on an idea by Penny, psycho-social direction by Lucinda, script supervised by Vera, with Duncan playing the lead part and engineered by everyone, was on the air.

LVII

The diary:

September 7, 506 A. L.

2:15 P.M.

The crowd is on the march! I can see them in the television monitor while I make my speech. But are they listening? For some reason they are tilting their radios upward and looking at the sky with amazed expressions. I have not yet told them to march on the Senate building.

2:30 P.M.

Messages are arriving from the southern, the northern and eastern regions. The army is suddenly immensely popular. Our occupying troops are being received with welcomes. Why? Can my speech have had that effect already? But the producer has just told me not half of it went out. It was interrupted by a news announcement. How could that be? Everyone is looking at me. I have just been handed another sheaf of messages.

Radio messages? Transmissions from the rocket? This is a hoax. They must broadcast that immediately.

3:00 P.M.

How did the Information Office succeed in this engineering? I am forced to think quickly. The whole planet is in turmoil. No one even knows the true position, and everything is rumor, hearsay, and stories no one can believe. One thing reported on the radio is that fighting has broken out between my desert troops and General Ilallah's Swamp Corps. This cannot be true, except as some minor skirmish of envy somewhere, yet by reporting it the news services are liable to make it true.

3:18 P.M.

This is pure disaster. Unaware of the state of preparation we are in, and because they are aware of some failure of communications, the government has ordered all army units and reservists to report to their regular stations. This completely cuts across every order we have issued. I have reports of units on the move held up by roads crowded with people fleeing from the cities on the reported threat of a space invasion. In other places, our men are welcomed with open arms, but that too delays them. Now the government edict cuts across all our orders, and the result is chaos.

The screen before me shows the leader of the Senate standing on the steps of the Senate building and haranguing an increasing crowd which completely blocks all roads and avenues in the vicinity. We were partly prepared for this, but not on this scale. This is a massive movement that seems engendered by some spontaneous instinct, and our troops, cut off by the crowd, and nominally engaged on crowd control, are getting contradictory orders. In the outskirts of the capital, and under the threat of invasion, our men are refusing to turn their arms on the common people, while in another section they are doing exactly that, but for the purposes of rape, or sacking shops, or looting.

LVIII

The Short History:

The revolution on Arcon that threw the Blues out of power and brought in the Greens would have happened anyway, but it was not that. A revolution is different in kind. It denotes some deeper change, and in this connection it is interesting to note the alterations in the unseen substructure. . . .

LIX

The Jottings:

While the messengers brought out the slips of paper from the lines, Lankowitz and I sat on the terrace of the mansion at Parker's Knoll and listened to the radio and looked at the sky beyond the creek and the jungle wall, where we expected the rocket to come down on the city like a flaming fireball.

We did not even take action to stop the mad woman who had evaded the cordon and who wandered around the lawn below us, then sat in the middle and apparently intended to have a picnic meal there.

"We must do something," I said, looking at each message as the messengers brought them in. "The situation is fluid, and if we don't do something, it will form itself."

But Lankowitz had stopped looking at the messages. "Do nothing," he said. "Haven't you learned anything yet? If you ever want to look foolish afterward, act first, in a time of crisis."

LX

The diary:

5:00 P.M.

A general knows what it is when his army begins to slip from his hands like grains of sand that drain away between the fingers, when they fraternize with the people, or kill them, but in any event do not obey their orders. Why has it happened, I ask myself, and again, why?

Is there something unknown in people, a romance, a desire to believe things, that is making people all over this planet believe against all sense and reason that they have an enemy in space out there? Or is there some desire, some senseless desire to go out into space, that began on Earth and has been latent here, so that the people only say they want to stay on Arcon, and build up the planet, and live the good life, while in their hearts they believe their destiny lies elsewhere, like the lemmings on Earth, who at certain seasons poured over cliffs to perish in the sea?

I do not understand it. This event has revealed a planet's madness. I see only the outward signs, the messages on my desk that come in from time to time. General Ilallah, suddenly and inexplicably, has issued a proclamation accusing me of a plot against the government and speaking of "unity in this hour of crisis." Our own agent, Pintopler 38239 - Z, has earned fame and self-importance by claiming that he saw "enemy vessels" on the radar screens at the time of the messages from Arcon One. There is no sense in these events, separated by a thousand miles of desert, and yet they make a pattern.

I do not only have papers in my desk. I have my gun there now.

Why have the people not believed in me, in my solid leadership?

What else is there?

I pick up my gun.

LXI

The Short History:

At such times it is easy for observers to be misled by the crowds in the streets, the hysteria, the shouting and the looting, the extravagant gestures of the orators, and the behavior of the soldiers. The people themselves do not know what they want at such times. They are "against" what has gone before, moving spontaneously, and often, it seems, without reason, motivated by no more than the heat on a summer's day. They do not know why they do what they do, except that they know that cracks have appeared in the façade of the world as it has seemed around them. What they wait for is someone who will create the new form.

Think of the language of the government leaders before and after the change of government. The Blue leader said:

"No responsible administrator of government finances could willingly countenance immoderate disposal of the planet's substance, however excellent the claims of the bio-chemical lobby may be, and indefatigably as the government will pursue a solution to our environmental problems."

The Green leader might have said the same before the revolution. After it, he said:

"We are men, and our men have guts. If the enemy comes here, we'll blast them. But that isn't enough. The road will be hard and tough, but we'll go and get them. We die soon enough not to care if we die a little sooner."

No one can explain how the people of Arcon, when it seemed that they had finally and officially accepted the fact of their early deaths, began slowly and surely to overcome the problem. They had the science, the intelligence before. Yet the will only came when they were looking not at their central problem but at something else, as though to overcome the difficulties, they had first to look beyond the problem.

LXII

The last private jottings of G. Berkeley:

I did not know how events were shaping. Sitting on the terrace of the mansion at Parker's Knoll, I did not know that I was about to see, as my last lesson, the human frailty of C. Q. Lankowitz. In the unaccustomed sunlit silence of our emergency retreat, I watched the blue iridescent air above the city beyond the jungle, and the messengers came and went while Lankowitz expressed the opinion that it was the fact that there were six girls in the rocket which had somehow caught the hearts and imagination of the Arcon people and caused riots around the planet.

"Surely not," I said, looking at the mad woman on the lawn as I saw how important it was, before we issued a statement, to judge the people's hearts and minds correctly. "What is moving them is fear, the fear of a space invasion."

"Who is she?" he said, seeing me looking at the figure on the lawn.

"Some woman who used to come here with her husband to use our lawn for picnics when the place was closed. They say she's crazy." I was surprised he gave her his attention.

"Why haven't the guards thrown her out?"

"They have. She won't tell them where the gap in the fence is, and when they throw her out she comes in again. She's harmless."

"Call her up," he said.

I did not realize at first what he wanted of her. Then I saw that the fact of her supposed madness was irrelevant to him. Most people were mad in his eyes, and to him she was the one member of the innocent public available to prove his point.

I went to the balustrade and called to her and waved.

She could not be expected to understand the motives for which we called her. She picked up her picnic basket and her transistor radio and came across the lawn and up the steps toward us.

"Who are you?" Lankowitz said in his friendly way, and waved her to the table.

"Mary Jean Smith," she said.

She put her open lunch on the table, and her radio beside her, looking at us as though she expected us to provide a drink to go with her lunch, while a planet burned.

Lankowitz indicated her radio. "What do you think of this space business?"

She looked as though she did not understand for a moment, then said, "Those poor girls."

Lankowitz wanted to encourage her to open her heart to us and give us the public reaction. He picked up one of her sandwiches and began to nibble it to show we were all good friends together. She watched him as though she had never seen a man eat a sandwich before.

"I put cyanide rat-poison in one of those this morning,"

she said. "I was going to kill myself and this seemed a better place than my flat to do it."

Lankowitz stopped eating and put his hand to his throat. After a while he bent over the table, and his body made strange contortions.

"No one comes to my flat now," Mary Jean Smith explained to me. "I would sooner be found in the open air than in a closed flat."

A messenger was coming out with a report slip. I sent him to get a doctor. Lankowitz was still dying, and I thought how inevitable it was that someone who knew everything, thought of everything, and allowed for everything, should fall over his own feet in some trivial mischance.

While a little crowd came out to surround the body, I looked away over the creeks and the jungle wall to the air above the city. There were greater events that we were seeing than the descent of the rocket like a fireball, and all because Lankowitz had made that other mistake of sending up a rocket under radio control but with an electronics man inside it.

I knew better then than to try to look after the Len Thomases of this or any other world within the cosmos, and I felt I was free from something. I turned around to seize control of the Information Office.

"Take down this statement that we will issue now," I told the clerks. "This Office confirms that for some time we have known that there was a threat from space to Arcon. The government accepts full responsibility for events, and is resigning because it has failed the Arcon people. The government in process of being formed is confident it can carry the war to Vista. You can add a note that our space heroes will be rescued by our first battle-cruisers on their way to Vista."

I looked at them blandly, and they stared at me. They knew as well as I did that a policy decision of that magnitude should be cleared with T. Chinn and P. Vulmany.

Especially as the government had not said it would resign yet.

But one of them had taken it down on his pad, and after looking silently at the others, he went to put it on the wires. "Go back to your work," I told them.

LXIII

SEEN FROM SPACE, the stars showed no sign of their view of events on Arcon.

"Success," Len said.

He looked at the small receiver they had made while they all sat and lay around in what might have been a temporary state of near-exhaustion. They were back on the couches and deck of the star dome, and the speaker of the receiver, which consisted of a telephone earpiece, made a thin piping sound. He switched it off. They knew now what was coming up from the newscasts of the planet away below them.

Salford looked out at the dark sky and the star field. He might have been counting the stars and galaxies, the quasars and galactic clouds. The pilot's console which had been in front of his couch had been dismantled in the course of their operations, and Salford did not say anything.

"We know too much to be taken back to Arcon," Ropotsky said. He looked at the tiny, silent bunch of wires as though it were speaking still. "They're going to have to take us on to Vista. When, is a different matter. If it takes them three years to build a starship, the time-difference can't make it less than a year in space for us."

A year in space was still a long time. Susan looked at her computer as though to work out the problem, then she stopped. To complete the radio network they had used the electronics of the computer too.

They looked at the stars around the rim of the dome. The last thing they had done before they stopped work was to make a meal. It looked as though there was nothing to stop them from going to their cabins.

Salford looked at Imantha. "It is our wedding night."

He was not the only man to look at his girl in that way, with a return of animation.

"Not just yet, it isn't," Vera said to Sorensen.

They sat still again. After a moment, they knew what they were waiting for. Len looked at Lucinda, and knew that everyone was looking in the same way.

"Lucinda," Duncan said.

Len felt for her. He looked at her slender shoulders and the curve of her back and waist as she sat on the couch beside him. She was his and he wondered if he could help her.

The chips were down now.

"Was it true, Lucinda?" Ed Creet said like the first accuser. "That method of thinking you told us that did not include 'impossible'?"

"Or a psycho-social operation on us?" Eliza Teen said.

The medical team had been thinking while they had been working.

What did they want? Len thought. *It had worked, hadn't it?* They had only to listen to the voices from the planet there below them.

Salford spoke almost silently into space. "Pure luck," he said. In the silence of space, they heard him.

Lucinda was looking at the deck and looking defensive when Salford spoke. Her eyes came up to him. "We are a team," she said. "Selected, all of us, by Yellows who believed in what they were doing, who were innocent of their leaders' betrayal and did their best. Do you think any leaders, any time, anywhere, can affect that?" It was the voice of the social-psychologist speaking.

Len thought of Berkelely and wondered if the word "innocent" could have been applied to him. In a way, he thought. In a distant way. But enough for what Lucinda said.

"I think Lucinda is prevaricating," Ropotsky said.

The beast with twenty-four legs was not united now, it seemed to Len. It had different heads and different features. Maybe it only appeared sometimes or when they had to have it.

Someone else broke the silence in the space dome. Len was surprised to hear Sorensen defend Lucinda.

"It just happened because we found a way to make it happen. Look at that universe out there around us." Sorensen pointed through the star dome.

"If you think you ever see and understand it, that is an illusion," he said. "Your eyes see only a narrow band of wavelengths. Your whole life is just a flash of galactic time. What you know of all that is hypothesis based on guess and superstition. What you think you know is only something you tell yourself about the way you learned to do things. Everything happens like that, and this happens to be an isolated way that we found."

Len saw Lucinda look at Duncan across the deck with a glance of gratitude.

To him? Len thought.

"Not isolated," he said. "Get it right. Arcon presented men with a psycho-social and organizational problem. Lucinda's branch of science happens to be the one that we produced because man came to Arcon. It represents the advance we have made."

Lucinda's glance came around to him, and he knew he had not said enough, not half enough. It was true that

158

something had happened, if not on Arcon then in the spaceship, that had something to do with communication and the structure of thought and man's internal organization too. He wished he knew.

Penny looked at Duncan and touched his hand. They were not going to grill Lucinda about how she did things, her look said, and Salford had been right when he had said it was their wedding night.

Susan looked out over the edge of the dome from the couch where she sat with Ropotsky. "Some people could make a mistake about that kind of thing," Susan said. It seemed she looked at distant worlds. "They might think that man could only improve physically, by mutation, like insects that have to be thrown away and die in droves for one advancement. But man improves with each problem he solves, and he will find one new problem with every new star."

Len wondered if anyone could be so foolish as to think that men would have to perish in millions now to make one new advancement. Even a computer, when it reached a certain level, could be taught to design new computers on a better mathematical frame than that. He did not think that any of the Yellow, intelligent fraction of humanity could fall for a mistake of that kind.

While waiting to see if anyone else said anything, he looked in the retro-view mirror at Arcon's disk, then away toward Vista and the stars beyond it.

Duncan responded to Penny's touch and look and got up. Before he turned to the spiral stair, he looked at them. "Who's going to volunteer to keep ship-watch on this deck tonight, while the rest of us are in our cabins?"

They had all begun to move when Duncan did, and then they stopped. *Don't all volunteer at once,* Len thought.

Lucinda said, "Len and I will."

Len wondered as he watched them all move and begin to go more quickly. They were heading for their cabins before he and Lucinda changed their minds about their offer. Yet they had all seen Lucinda work. They knew what she was capable of. Sometimes, it just did not register.

When the others had gone, and the last head had disappeared down the hatchway in the deck, Len began to collect loose equipment and put it to one side. There was some talk and slamming of doors below. When it stopped, he went to the stairhead. Then he began to put the loose equipment on the stair. Thoughtfully, he tied a notice to it.

Lucinda was releasing the foam rubber from the blast-off

couches, and laying a square of it, eight feet by six, in the center of the deck. She looked a little shy when Len caught her eye. "It's more spacious up here," she said. "And besides, the view is better."

"I know," Len said. "And if the watchkeeper were to see anything in space tonight, he couldn't do a thing about it."

Salford had said their luck was good, and as Len undressed under the immense hemisphere of heavens above the dome, he knew that this night they would have to rely on it, until tomorrow, when the control equipment could be reassembled. Then Len stopped thinking of things like that entirely.

It was the sight of Lucinda, naked, with the starlight gleaming on her hair and figure, and her toes barely touching the deck in the light gravity of the starship as she came toward him. He had not realized that that too was something she had thought of.

It was not long before what Len saw of the universe was its reflection in miniature in Lucinda's dark eyes.

"After all, the stars have seen this kind of thing before," she told him.